PROMISE

to

Marry

JESSICA WOOD

This book is a work of fiction. Names, characters, places, and incidents either are the product of the author's imagination or are used fictitiously. Any resemblance to actual persons, living or dead, events, or locales is entirely coincidental.

ISBN-13: 978-1507514511

ISBN-10: 1507514514

First Edition: January 2015

Also by Jessica Wood

Emma's Story Series

- *A Night to Forget* – Book One
- *The Day to Remember* – Book Two
- *Emma's Story* Box Set – Contains Book One & Book Two

The Heartbreaker Series

This is an *Emma's Story* spin-off series featuring Damian Castillo, a supporting character in *The Day to Remember*. This is a standalone series and does not need to be read with *Emma's Story* series.

- *Damian* – Book One
- *The Heartbreaker* – Prequel Novella to *DAMIAN* – can be read before or after *Damian.*
- *Taming Damian* – Book Two

- *The Heartbreaker Box Set* – Contains all three books.

The Chase Series

This is a standalone series with cameo appearances from Damian Castillo (*The Heartbreaker series*).

- *The Chase, Vol. 1*
- *The Chase, Vol. 2*
- *The Chase, Vol. 3*
- *The Chase, Vol. 4*
- *The Chase: The Complete Series Box Set* – Contains All Four Volumes

Oblivion

This is a standalone full-length book unrelated to other series by Jessica Wood.

- *Oblivion*

***

Pre-Orders Currently Available

- *Promise to Keep* – February 9, 2015

PROMISE

to

"Hope is the thing with feathers that perches in the soul - and sings the tunes without the words - and never stops at all."

Emily Dickinson

Prologue

When we first met twenty-three years ago, I had hated him.

"You look like Pippi Longstocking!" That was the very first thing he'd said to me. He'd flashed me a boyish grin as he pointed to the pigtails my mom had braided for me that morning before I had said goodbye to her.

I'd stuck my tongue out at him in protest as I followed Aunt Betty and Uncle Tom into their house—my new home. I had known instantly that I wouldn't like this boy. He was mean, he was a bully, and he sure wasn't going to be any friend of mine.

Well, at least that was what I had thought that day when I moved in with Aunt Betty and her husband. But, like so many other things I'd thought throughout my life, I had been wrong.

Somehow, despite my resistance, he'd chipped away at my stone-cold seven-year-old exterior and won me over within a matter of just a week. I'd discovered that he wasn't mean after all. He wasn't a bully, either. In fact, somehow, without even knowing how it'd happened, he had quickly become my friend—and not just any old friend—he had become my best friend. My confidant. My constant. My anchor.

We'd been inseparable as we grew up together, spending hours in his treehouse, talking and laughing until Aunt Betty would call me into the house for bed every night.

And even in one of my darkest hour when I was thirteen—when I felt the most lost and alone, when I purposely drove everyone, including him, away—he had been there, by my side, to comfort me. He had been my rock and had refused to be ignored or pushed away.

That was the day we had made our pact: If we were still single by the time we were thirty, we'd marry each other.

I had known even then just how lucky I had been to have him in my life. I had loved him the way best friends loved each other. But it wasn't until I had lost him that I had realized just how much I'd love him—how much my love for him went far beyond friendship. It wasn't until we were no longer friends that I had realized that he had been my one and only love all along.

But by then, it was too late. I had screwed up. I had ruined everything. I had done something that was unforgivable. And a part of me wondered if I had enjoyed it. So how could I possibly ask him to forgive me when I couldn't forgive myself?

Now, twenty-three years after we'd first met, we were both thirty and single, but I knew that it was he who now hated me.

Chapter One

Present Day

"Promise?" I looked into his rich, emerald eyes—those eyes that always had a way of making me feel at home.

"Promise." He beamed at me and squeezed my hands as we secured the love-lock onto the bridge railing and locked it in place.

He pulled me into his arms and whispered in my ear, "You're my best friend, Clo. You won't ever have to worry about being alone. I promise that I'll always be here for you when you need me."

A splendid mixture of bliss and comfort spread through me like a warm blanket on a cold day as I sank into his inviting embrace. Despite everything that'd happened in my life, I felt hopeful. Because I knew that no matter what the future held for me, Jackson would always be there. And for me, that was enough.

"Here's to your thirtieth birthday," he said playfully as he finally pulled away.

"And yours too," I added.

"Well, not exactly." He paused and grinned—that same boyish grin from the first day we met, the same boyish grin I'd come to know so well in the past eleven years, the same boyish grin that made my heart soar with happiness.

"What do you mean?" I feigned a frown, knowing too well he was being a smart-ass.

"Well, seeing as I'm eight months older than you, our pact won't start when I turn thirty." He chuckled smugly. *"So I'm rooting for your thirtieth."*

"Jax."

The sound of my own voice woke me from my dream. My eyelids felt heavy as I tried to open them and keep them open, battling against the inviting weight of sleep. Finally, I gave in and closed my eyes again, a part of me hoping I'd drift back into that memory from years ago, a memory that seemed as vivid as if it'd happened just yesterday.

But it was too late. The dream was gone. I couldn't return back to that moment in time—back to that moment with *him*.

I opened my eyes, drawing in a long inhale of breath as reality set in. Today was my thirtieth birthday. The big 3-0! I'd always thought that when this day finally came, I'd somehow feel different. I thought that this day would *feel* meaningful, that somehow a magical switch would turn on inside me and I'd have it all figured it.

I was wrong. I didn't feel any different this morning than I had the night before. Nothing had changed. I was still working at my boring administrative assistant job at a law firm, living in a tiny studio apartment in a shitty neighborhood in downtown Los Angeles, and getting by, paycheck to paycheck. This wasn't how I had envisioned my life to be at thirty. *Because he isn't in it*, a tiny voice said inside.

Feeling a bit frustrated with myself, I kicked off the comforter and walked to the bathroom to splash some cold water on my face.

"You're being ridiculous, Chloe," I said out loud to the reflection that stared back at me from the mirror above the sink. "You're overreacting. You don't have a miserable life. In fact, it's pretty damn good. You just had a weird dream and now you're being irrationally nostalgic." I splashed some more water against my face, trying to wake myself up so I could think clearly. Drawing a deep, labored breath, I looked back into the mirror and spoke again, but this time I spoke as if I were trying to persuade someone off a ledge. "That's all in the past. You can't change it. You can't. The only thing you can do is move forward. You have a lot to look forward to."

I grabbed a towel and patted off the water from my face. "You're right," I responded back to my reflection and flashed a resolute smile. "I have so much to be happy about. I'm thirty and I have a wonderful boyfriend who makes me happy and takes care of me."

Just then, as if in support of my positive thinking, my phone started ringing. It was Carly.

"*And* I have a new best friend, and here she is now."

Feeling a lot better than moments ago, I grabbed my phone and answered it.

"Hi, Carly," I said cheerfully.

Before I could stop here, Carly's musically-challenged voice came through the phone as she sang me "Happy Birthday" off-key with such confidence, you'd think that was how all people sang the song if you hadn't known any better.

I burst into a fit of laughter. "Thanks for that. I really needed a good laugh this morning."

"Hey, everyone loves my incredible off-pitch renditions of songs. I'm simply giving them the Carly-twist." I could hear the humor in her voice as she pretended to sound serious.

"And I, for one, love the Carly-twist," I played along.

"Well naturally," she said sarcastically in her diva voice.

I giggled as I pictured her flipping her long blond waves over her shoulder as she batted her long lashes.

"So how does it feel to be *so* old?" she teased.

"No different than I felt yesterday. But don't worry, you'll find out for yourself in a few short months," I teased back.

"Touché." She groaned. "Get those old-lady walkers ready for me."

I laughed and shook my head. "You're too much sometimes, Carly."

"Oh, you love it."

"Riiight." I dragged out the word, highlighting the sarcasm in my voice.

"So what do you have planned today? Will I even get to see you?"

"Well, Jeff's taking me out for dinner and this comedy show tonight."

"Ohhh, that sounds like fun. So are you going into work today or taking the day off?"

"I'm working today. I want to save my vacation days and can't afford to take a non-paid day off."

"Girl, you seriously work too hard. You need to live a little. It's your *thirtieth* birthday, and you have a self-employed boyfriend who works from home. What you *should* be doing today is having lots of obligatory birthday-sex with your hot sex-on-a-stick boyfriend."

I laughed. "All you think about is sex."

"True story. It's the gift that keeps on giving."

"You're seriously too much sometimes, Carly." I giggled.

"Thank you," she said proudly.

I rolled my eyes. In the past two years I'd known Carly, she'd always been that free-spirited wild child, the type of girl that I'd dreamt about being, but knew I could never emulate even if I'd tried.

"Anyway, babe," she continued, "I gotta get going now, but I wanted to wish you a happy birthday."

"Thanks, Carly. Maybe we can grab lunch today near the office?" Carly and I worked only two blocks from one another, so we tried to meet up for lunch at least once a week.

"Yeah, maybe a late lunch? I have a business meeting out of the office this morning, so I probably won't be back in the office until one."

"Sure. How about one-thirty, then? And if you're running late, just let me know."

"Sounds like a plan. Have a good day at work, babe. See you soon."

"Thanks, Carly. And don't worry, I'll be sure to make time for that birthday sex."

She laughed. "Get it, girl!" With that, she clicked off.

***

"Thank you, Mr. O'Brien. I'm sorry this was so last minute."

"Don't worry about it, Chloe," my boss reassured. "It's been a slow week at the office anyway. Have a nice birthday and enjoy the day off."

A huge smile spread across my face when I got off the phone. After my conversation with Carly a few minutes before, I realized that she was absolutely right. I had to live a little. It was my thirtieth birthday. I had a gorgeous boyfriend who had a flexible schedule. Why shouldn't I treat myself to a day off work and spend the day having birthday sex?

With a renewed sense of excitement, I'd completely pushed my dream from this morning out of my thoughts as I raced to my closet to find something to wear. I reached for my phone to tell him I was coming over, but before I pulled up his name, I decided that I wanted to surprise him instead.

Surprise sex for him. Birthday sex for me. Win-win. I felt giddy with excitement as I riffled through my clothes. After a few seconds of searching, my fingers stopped dead in their tracks when they found the perfect outfit. A devious smirk curled my lips as I quickly grabbed it from the hanger and got ready.

Thirty minutes later, I was standing outside his apartment in nothing but a sleek black trench coat that came down mid-thigh and a pair of black five-inch fuck-me boots.

I felt sexy, adventurous, and aroused as I knocked on his door, anticipating the things we'd do to each other, the things he'd do to me. Jeff may not have been perfect in many ways, but when it came to sex, he was pretty damn close.

When he didn't answer the door, I knocked again. Still no response. I leaned my head on the door and could hear what sounded like the TV from the other side. *He must be working at his office desk in his bedroom.*

Just then I remembered that Jeff had given me a set of his keys for those in-case-of-emergency situations.

Is the need for birthday sex on your big 3-0 considered an emergency? "Close enough," I decided out loud as I pulled out his keys.

When I walked into the living room, I could hear the muffled sounds of cries and a struggle coming from the TV in the bedroom.

I laughed when I realized what Jeff must be watching and walked through the hallway leading to the bedroom.

"Jeff, are you watching *Jerry Springer* again? I knew you secretively loved that—" But when I walked into the room, my words got lost in my throat as shock paralyzed me in place at what I saw.

There, on the cream sheepskin area rug I'd gotten him last Christmas, was Jeff, naked and on his knees, pounding himself in and out of some blonde's ass.

"Chloe!" Jeff called out in alarm. He leaped off the woman, his erection emerging from inside the blonde. It wasn't until that moment that the woman turned around, causing a sharp gasp to escape my lips.

She wasn't some random woman. She wasn't some stranger. She was none other than *Carly*, my best friend.

I felt like the oxygen had been sucked out of the room and replaced with something more dense and threatening. For what seemed like eternity, we just stood there, staring at each other in wide-eyed shock, both unable to say a thing.

"I—I can explain!" Jeff stammered out as he moved toward me, causing his still-hard erection to point straight at me, almost as if to ask me to look at it and acknowledge where it'd just been.

"*Don't* touch me!" I screamed as I backed away from him. I glared at him, then Carly, and then back to him. "I don't understand. How could you guys? My boyfriend? My best friend?" I drew in a sharp, uneven breath. "And on my fucking birthday?"

"Chloe," Carly's voice was soft, almost pleading, "I'm sorry. We didn't intentionally want to hurt you…"

"Shut up, Carly! Just shut the fuck up! What was all that bullshit this morning about making sure I got my birthday sex from Jeff today, and how I should take the day off? And when I decide to take your advice, take the day off and come see him, I walk in on *you* fucking him! Did I miss something? Is *your* name

Chloe? Did *you* turn thirty today? Is he *your* boyfriend?" By this point, I was fuming with rage.

"I—I didn't know you'd show up, Chloe," she pleaded. "I asked you this morning what your plans were today. You said you'd be at work. I didn't plan for you to see this."

I snorted at her attempt to reason with herself. "Oh, so that makes it okay for you to fuck your best friend's boyfriend? Because you didn't *know* I'd find out?"

I watched her open her mouth to respond but then she closed it without saying a word.

Jeff moved toward me again. This time, he grabbed one of my hands and forced me to face him.

"Chloe, I love you. This was just a mistake. It doesn't change the way I feel about you."

I stared at him in utter disbelief. "Do you really think this doesn't change things between us? Do you really think I can just forget this happened—that I can forget everything I just saw? Because trust me, if I could scrub the images of you fucking my friend in the ass from my memory, I'd ask you to go get me some bleach and a scrub brush."

"Please, Chloe. Baby?" He flashed me an innocent frown.

"Fuck you, Jeff! *Don't* you 'baby' me!"

"Come on, let's talk about this," he persisted.

"Get your head out of your ass, Jeff—or her ass for that matter! Don't you get it? There's nothing to talk about. We're over!" I yanked my hand from his grasp and ran for his front door. I ran as fast as I could until I reached the safety of my car. It wasn't until I drove away from his building that the anger evaporated away and tears took its place as they streamed down my face.

I cried the entire way home. And as my mind raced with a million thoughts, there was one that seemed to resonate in my head more so than any other.

It's karma. After almost a year of eluding it, it's finally caught up to me, and I deserve every painful moment of it.

Chapter Two

Present Day

I was on a bender.

I was on the reckless path leading to self destruction.

I was completely and utterly lost.

But the thing was, I didn't care.

This was what I wanted.

This was the only way I knew how to mentally escape from everything.

This was how fucked up I was.

Tonight was yet another night I'd found myself at the neighborhood dive bar on Hollywood Boulevard. Much like the previous nights this week, I'd gotten home after work, absentmindedly ate whatever takeout I'd grabbed on the way home, took a few vodka shots in the kitchen—to save money, of course—before walking the four blocks to the bar to close out the night in a blurry haze.

It was just a little before nine when I got to the bar tonight. It was a Friday, so the place was much more crowded than the previous nights. *More options and no work in the morning*, I thought to myself. I walked straight to the bar when I arrived and waved the bartender over.

"Hey, there. Chloe, right?"

"Yup, that's me. Hey…?" I tilted my head toward him slightly, signaling for him to remind me of his name. Who could possibly keep track of names when you were just a few drinks away from being three sheets to the wind?

"Steve." He flashed me his perfect pearly whites as he wiped down the counter between us. *Wannabe actor*, I immediately thought. Living in Los Angeles, you could spot them from a mile away.

"Right. Hi, Steve."

"So what are we having tonight?"

"A glass of vodka, dirty, and a shot of Bacardi 151, hold the judgment."

He smirked at me. "So the usual?" I wasn't sure why, but his smug comment bothered me.

I didn't answer him. But instead of waiting for a response, he went to make them, clearly taking my silence as a yes. A minute later, he was back with my drinks.

"Tough day?" He placed the glasses in front of me and looked at me with half-interest.

"How about tough *week*?" I corrected him as I threw back the shot of 151 and chased it down with a healthy gulp of vodka.

"Whoa there." Steve raised his eyebrows, his eyes widening slightly with surprise. "Honey, you'd better slow your roll if you want to remember anything in the morning."

"Didn't I say 'hold the judgment?'" I challenged him, feeling agitated by how he looked at me with unease, like I was some unstable person who needed help. *It's not like he hasn't seen me drink the previous nights.*

Okay fine, so maybe I was a little unstable, and maybe I did need help. But he was the bartender. I was paying him to make me my drinks, not to be my shrink.

To my relief, Steve had no time to respond. A group of girls at the far end of the bar waved him down, and he seemed relieved to leave our conversation to go take their drink orders.

As I sat there and sipped my vodka, something from the corner of my eye caught my attention. A girl with electric-blue hair had just walked through the front door and was waving to a group of people sitting at a booth on the opposite end of the bar. It wasn't this particular girl, nor the color of her hair that I was drawn to. It was the red heart-shaped lock secured around the strap of her messenger bag that had caused my body to tense up.

"Ugh. I don't want to think about him," I muttered under my breath as I peeled my eyes off the red lock. But the harder I tried to not think about him, the more thoughts of him that began to surface in the forefront of my mind. *Jax.* I downed the rest of my vodka, trying to drown out my thoughts. "I want to think about *anything* but him right now."

"Why don't you think about me instead?" came a voice from right behind me.

The closeness of his voice alarmed me momentarily, but I recovered quickly and turned to face the stranger who had just walked up to the bar and sat down on the stool next to mine. He flashed me a meaningful smile and I gave him a quick once-over before returning my gaze to my empty glass. He looked to be in his mid-twenties and was cute enough for my purposes.

"And why exactly should I think about you?" I challenged in my flirtatious voice.

"Well, a sexy lady like you shouldn't be drinking alone and *not* thinking about me."

I raised an eyebrow but didn't turn back to look at him right away. I liked that he was cocky and had more confidence about himself than he should probably possess. He was exactly what I was looking for tonight.

When I finally turned to meet his salivating gaze, I knew by the way he looked at me that this was going to be too easy.

"Well, you're wrong. I'm not drinking alone tonight." For a second, his face fell. "—because I'm drinking with you."

His face immediately lit up like a Christmas tree in December and he inched his seat closer to mine. There was a greedy lust in his eyes, and I knew to him, this was probably his lucky night, where a sleazy pick-up line actually worked for a change. But to me, I just needed to forget.

"So what would you like to drink?"

"Another glass of vodka, dirty."

"Dirty," he repeated. "I like that." He smirked and licked his lips.

"I'm sure you do," I shot back sarcastically.

"You're feisty." He laughed and motioned Steve over. I avoided Steve's gaze, not wanting to see any hint of judgment in his eyes. I was on a good buzz, and I didn't need it to be ruined by reality.

"So my name's Brent. What's yours?"

"C—" I paused for a second. "Carly." I grinned over at him. All I wanted to do tonight was to forget about who I was. It seemed fitting in more ways than one to use her name.

When the drinks came, I grabbed mine and downed half the glass without bothering to wait for the guy.

He chuckled as he reached for his drink. "I love a woman who can appreciate a good, stiff drink."

Feeling tired of this forced banter, I moved my hand under the bar counter. When I found the growing bulge in his jeans, I leaned over and whispered so only he could hear, "That's not the only stiff thing I can appreciate."

That not-so-subtle invitation was all it took. Minutes later, before he had a chance to even taste his drink, we were in the men's bathroom where he had me pinned up against the wall in the last stall.

"Fuck me hard," I demanded as his hands frantically removed my black mini-dress over my head and threw it over the stall door. "I want it rough and painful."

"You're a bad girl, aren't you, Carly?" he growled in my ear, the heat of his breath sending a mixture of anticipation and disgust to run down my body. But I knew I couldn't stop. I knew I wanted to stop thinking. I knew I needed this escape, now more than ever. I closed my eyes and felt the alcohol numbing my body as his hungry mouth pressed hard against mine and his hands began to massage my breasts. I gasped and moaned at all the appropriate moments, but my heart wasn't in it. It was as if I was having an out-of-body experience and I was watching an up-close porno. My body didn't resist as his moved down to my breasts, his tongue flicking my nipples as his hand disappeared down between my legs, his fingers exploring the depths of my wetness. I heard myself cry out in pleasure as his slightly-curled fingers moved in and out of me, causing my legs to buckle under me.

Then he pulled out of me and sucked my juices from his fingers as he dropped his pants and slipped on a condom. I could see from the hungry frenzy in his eyes that there was no turning back.

"You want it rough, baby?" His ragged voice was dark and threatening.

"Yes," I heard myself beg.

Suddenly he lifted my legs off the ground, and I felt his erection rub against my entrance. "God, you're so fucking wet," he groaned in a hoarse voice.

I was about to respond, but it was too late. Instead, I cried out in both pain and pleasure as I felt him plunge all the way inside me, not holding back a single inch of him. I dug my nails deep into the muscular hardness of his back as each of his violent thrusts went deeper and harder than the last. Through my half-opened eyes, I saw his face twisted in pleasure as uncontrollable gasps and moans escaped my lips.

A few minutes later, we finally climaxed, taking me to the peak of pleasure and oblivion. In that split second, my mind was completely free from the shackles of my thoughts. But as quickly as it came, it also left, and as I pulled up my panties and adjusted the dress on my body, reality began to creep its way back into my consciousness.

"Fuck, that was incredible," he growled in a husky voice as he leaned forward to nuzzle against my neck.

I cringed and averted his touch and reached for the bathroom-stall door.

"Where are you going with that sexy ass of yours?"

I felt a little dizzy and sick but turned back to face him. When our eyes met, I realized that I had just let a complete stranger fuck me in a disgusting bathroom stall, and it wasn't until after our dirty act that I'd actually looked at him clearly for the first time.

Why did I do this, again?

To escape the pain you fell in your heart, I heard a small voice respond inside me.

But escaping the pain was short-lived. Not even the empty bliss of an orgasm could keep it at bay for too long. I felt my body waking up from the pain-numbing effects of ecstasy and I knew I needed to get out of here before things got worse.

As I started to pull the stall door open to leave, his hand found mine and pulled me back inside. Before I could pull away, he guided my hand down to his already-hard erection.

"How about another round?"

I looked away, cringing inside at what I had just done with this stranger. "Sorry. I gotta go, Bryan," I said as I finally managed to pull my hand out of his grip. I quickly opened the door and stumbled out of the stall.

"It's Brent."

"What?" I looked back at him, realizing he had just said something to me. My mind was somewhere else—already running away from this mistake.

"My name is Brent, not Bryan."

I sighed. "Look. I really don't care. I'm not looking for anything serious here. If I was, I probably wouldn't have let you fuck me in the men's bathroom at a bar after meeting you for less than five minutes." Shame consumed me when I realized that I had just slept with another man I had no feelings for.

"Oh, don't be like that," he teased. "We can still go back out to the bar, have a few more drinks, and then take the party back to my place for a night cap."

"Trust me," I said almost inaudibly as I turned away from him, "you don't want anything to do with me."

Regret gripped my insides as I ran out of the bathroom without waiting for him to respond.

Turning thirty had rattled me more than I wanted to admit. I wanted to blame it on the events of last week—blame Jeff for cheating on me, blame Carly for being a shitty friend, blame my luck for having it all happen to me on my thirtieth birthday. But I knew deep down there was something more to my unhappiness. I knew it had nothing to do with Jeff, or even Carly. I knew it was something that had been brewing over the past nine years. What happened with Jeff and Carly was only the trigger, the tip of the iceberg. But they weren't the iceberg. They weren't the root of the immense pain I'd bottled up inside, a pain that'd pressed against my chest, unable to find its release.

Chapter Three

Present Day

By the time I stumbled into my apartment, I felt like shit. I felt dirty. I felt more alone than I'd ever remembered feeling. All the drinks I'd had in the last few hours crashed down on me all at once and I felt myself start to unravel emotionally. I knew I shouldn't fixate on the one thing—the one person—who could push me further down this rabbit hole, but it was too late.

In my drunken stupor, I pulled up Facebook and typed his name in the search box: "Jackson Pierce." He was the first result. We had twenty-one mutual friends. But we weren't friends. He'd de-friended me after that day. I hovered the cursor over his name and hesitated. I knew there would be no turning back once I clicked through. I knew I'd want to look through everything. Twice. I knew this wasn't healthy for me. But it was just too hard to resist. I was like a kid who was left in a room alone and told not to look inside the shiny box full of toys. *I have to look! This is killing me*, I convinced myself.

Before I could snap to my senses, I clicked on his name. In a blink of an eye, I was staring straight at his profile picture. His olive complexion, his rich, emerald eyes, his warm smile—he looked more handsome than I'd remembered, and he looked happy as his photo smiled back at me. I smiled back and traced the outline of his face with my fingers. For the next hour, I felt myself tumbling down the bottomless rabbit hole as I combed through his Facebook page, looking through every status, every comment, every photo. I tried to soak up everything I could about his life, trying to imagine myself in it, trying to imagine how my life would be if we were still friends—if I hadn't destroyed our friendship.

"I'm sorry, Jax," I whispered to his photo. "If I could go back and do things differently, I wouldn't have hurt you. I would have figured out another way through the mess."

Against my better judgment, I stumbled over to my bookshelf and riffled through a box of CDs on the bottom shelf. As soon as I found what I was searching for, I pulled it out and pushed it into the CD slot of my sound system. It was a CD Jax had made for me a decade ago when we were in college. I never knew why I hadn't realized then how he'd felt about me, but every song on the CD made it perfectly clear that he wanted to be more than friends, that he wanted the same thing I'd wanted for us but was too scared to hope for. I fast-forwarded to my favorite track on the playlist, Jeff

Buckley's "Lover, You Should've Come Over," and programmed it to play on a repeated loop.

I slumped down on the couch, suddenly feeling physically and emotionally drained. As the guitar strummed the melancholy melody and Jeff Buckley's deep voice sang the hypnotic song about young lovers and regret, tears began to stream down my face. I'd tried for a long time to hide from the truth, to ignore my true feelings for him, but tonight, after I'd lost everything that seemed to have had any value to me, there were no more walls I could hide behind.

I missed him. I'd missed him for a very long time now. Deeply. Desperately. Painfully. I missed him to the point where it'd become hard to breathe. I would give anything for us to be best friends again. I would give anything for him to be here by my side right now like he'd promised me years ago when I felt lonely. Tears continued to stream down my face as the song radiated through me and the lyrics hit home, speaking straight to my heart and how I was feeling about him.

Just then I sat straight up on the couch. "Maybe it's not too late," I said out loud as I responded to a line in the lyrics. "Maybe we're like this song and we were just too young for anything good to happen between us? But now we're older…"

Before I knew what I was doing, I pulled up the number I'd had of his from years ago and pressed the call button before I could change my mind.

After two rings, he picked up and I heard his half-awake voice mumble, "Hello?"

I drew in a deep breath, ready to tell him everything, that I was sorry, that I'd missed him, that I was thirty and single, and the only person I wanted to be with was him. But nothing came out of my mouth. I felt paralyzed by fear.

"Hello?" I heard him say again, this time sounding louder and more awake.

Suddenly, in a moment of clarity, I panicked and ended the call without saying a word. What was I thinking calling him in the middle of the night when I was wasted, reckless, and emotionally unstable? We hadn't talked or seen each other since that day nine years ago. Nothing good could come out of a late-night drunken phone call right now.

I let out a groan and slumped back onto the couch. It was then that the pile of bills and junk mail I had thrown on the coffee table several days earlier caught my attention. There, in the middle of the stack, was a thick, large, ivory card-stock envelope. I reached over and plucked it from the pile. I didn't have to open it to know that it was a wedding invitation. I glanced at the return address.

Mr. and Mrs. Montgomery

6843 Lester Court

West Chester, Pennsylvania

West Chester. That was where I grew up with Aunt Betty and Uncle Tom. But who were the Montgomerys?

Then it hit me. Clara Montgomery. The always-bubbly and high-spirited girl from high school.

She had been in the same circle of friends with me and Jax. I hadn't talked to her in over two years, and that was when I had randomly run into her on a quick trip home to visit Aunt Betty and Uncle Tom after I had been abroad for five years and before I'd moved to Los Angeles.

I smiled. She had always been nice to me, the eternal optimist in our group. I was glad to see she'd found happiness. As I read the wedding invitation, I wondered if Jax was going to go to Clara's wedding this summer. A jolt of anxious nerves shot through me as I imagined seeing him again, after all this time, after everything that had happened. Hundreds of questions invaded my mind. What would I say to him? What would he say to me? Was he single? Did he miss me? Could he forgive me? Was there a way things could go back to the way they were? With all the questions I had, my mind seemed to always return to the same one: Did he remember our pact?

While "Lover, You Should've Come Over" continued to play in the background, I drifted in and out of consciousness. My living room slowly slipped away and was replaced with a familiar off-white ceiling that glowed with a kaleidoscope of magical lights. I felt his sweaty hand holding mine as he smiled over at me. *This is where we made our pact. This is where he first kissed me. This is where I want to be.*

And right before I was completely engulfed by sleep, I heard myself mutter, "Jax … I'm single … I hope you are too …"

Chapter Four

Summer 1992

Seven Years Old

"You be a good girl, you hear, baby?" My mom brushed through the knots in my chestnut-brown hair, preparing to put it in pigtail braids.

"I will, Mommy." I tried to turn and smile up at her. I knew she thought I always wanted her to braid my hair because I liked it in pigtails. But that wasn't it. I thought pigtails made me look like a silly kid, and I didn't want to look like a kid. I needed to grow up, so that I could take care of us both.

I actually never liked my hair in pigtails at all. But I never told my mom that. The real reason I always wanted her to braid my hair was because it was one of my favorite things to do with her. It was when she would talk to me without being distracted, when she wasn't on the phone talking about money, when she wasn't crying or angry. And because she needed to use both hands to braid my hair, she couldn't smoke or drink either, and I knew that was good for her.

When my mom would braid my hair, she seemed happier as well. She would smile and hum to herself, and I loved it when she smiled. It made her look so beautiful, and it made me feel warm and happy inside.

But today felt different.

I couldn't see her as she stood behind me, but I could tell that something was wrong today. She wasn't smiling or humming today. "You don't have to worry about me, Mommy." I tried to stay positive and happy for her.

"You need to always listen to what Aunt Betty and Uncle Tom tell you to do, okay?" There was an unusual crack in her voice that made me sad, but I wasn't quite sure why I felt that way.

"I will. I promise. Cross my heart and hope to fly. Stick a beetle in my pie."

Suddenly, my mom started to laugh, but it wasn't her normal laugh. This sounded like she was laughing and crying at the same time.

I turned around and looked up at her in confusion. "What's wrong, Mommy? Why are you laughing funny?"

"You're just the sweetest girl any mommy can have, baby." She beamed at me, and for a brief moment, her normal, blood-shot eyes looked clear and focused. She leaned down and planted a gentle kiss on my forehead, which instantly made me giggle with delight.

"That tickles, Mommy!" But my mom didn't seem to hear me correctly, because she started to tickle me on both sides of my stomach, causing me to squeal and laugh, and I begged her to stop.

Finally, when my stomach hurt so much from giggling that I could barely breathe, she finally let me go.

"All right, enough fooling around, honey. Aunt Betty and Uncle Tom will be here soon. So if you still want me to braid your hair, then you have to stay still."

"Okay, Mommy. I'll be good."

As she braided my hair, I brushed through my Belle Barbie's brown hair, mimicking my mom's movements. I smiled and kissed Belle on the cheek. She was my first and only doll. She was my best friend. I could still remember when I got her last Christmas. I had felt like the luckiest girl in the world when I opened the wrapped package. My mom said a secret

Santa got it for me. She said that I had been a very good girl last year, and Santa wanted to give me something special this year. She was right. Belle was really special.

"Mommy?" I looked back up at her as she secured the hair-tie ball at the end of one of the braids.

"Yes, honey?"

"Do you know if there are books at Aunt Betty and Uncle Tom's house?"

"Why do you ask that?"

I held Belle Barbie up so my mom could see her. "Belle likes to read books. When she was living with the Beast, there was a library in his castle, so she was really happy. Aunt Betty and Uncle Tom's house is big like a castle. Does that mean they have a library too?"

My mom smiled down at me. "I can't remember if they do, but there's a library nearby that I'm sure Aunt Betty can take you and Belle to if you ask. Doesn't that sound wonderful?"

I grinned up at her and nodded enthusiastically. "Belle will like that a lot."

"You and Belle will be really happy there." Her voice sounded sad again.

I frowned, wondering if I had said something that made her upset.

"Mommy, how come you're not moving to Aunt Betty's with us?" I looked back up at her and made myself smile. I didn't understand why, but I knew my mom was very sad, and I needed to be brave so she wouldn't worry about me.

My mom didn't respond right away. "Honey, you've asked me that before."

"I know, Mommy. Sorry I don't remember what you said." I felt bad for lying to her, but I didn't want to tell her that when I had asked her the other day, she had forgotten to tell me.

I heard her let out a deep sigh before she turned me around to look up at her. "Chloe, you're a big girl now, and you deserve to know what is happening. So I will tell you something important, okay?"

I nodded.

When she bent down to face me, I could smell the usual stale remnants of alcohol on her breath mixed in with her morning cigarette. "Honey, Mommy is sick." She paused and I saw some tears in her eyes. "For a long time, Mommy didn't want to admit to herself that she was sick, but she is. And because she's sick, she hasn't been taking care of her baby girl the way a good mommy should."

Her words scared me. "Are you going to die, Mommy?" I tried as hard as I could to hold back the tears that burned my eyes. I had to be strong for her. I had to be strong for the both of us. But I couldn't do it. I couldn't stop my body from shaking as I started to cry. I buried my face in her chest and held on to her as tightly as I could.

"Shh, honey," she crooned as she held me. "It'll be okay. I'm not going to die."

I pulled my face from her chest and sniffled. "You promise?"

She nodded and smiled. "I'm going to get better, baby. I'm going to a place where they'll help me get better."

"How long will you be gone?"

She shrugged. "I'm not sure. It can be a long recovery process."

"Oh." I bowed my head and looked at the floor, trying to think about what she was saying. "Can Belle and I come too?" I looked up at her hopefully.

"No, I'm sorry, honey. It's a place just for sick people to get better. That's why you're going to be living with Aunt Betty and Uncle Tom. You'll be happy there."

I shook my head and pouted. I wasn't happy with what I was hearing. "Mommy, I can pretend to be sick like you. That way I can be with you and take care of you. I can be really good at pretending. Please, Mommy? I just want to be where you are."

"I really wish you could come too, baby, but you can't. There are good people who protect kids like you and they think that Aunt Betty and Uncle Tom can take care of you better right now." Tears streamed down her face, which made me very sad.

"Please don't cry, Mommy." I reached up and wiped away her tears with my fingers. "I didn't mean to upset you. I will be a big girl for you, Mommy. I'll take care of Belle and I'll listen to everything Aunt Betty and Uncle Tom tell me to do. I'll be a good girl. Please don't be upset with me."

She smiled, but her eyes didn't twinkle like they usually did when she smiled at me.

But before I could ask any more questions, there was a knock at the door, causing us both to jump in surprise.

"All right, that must be them, Chloe." My mom pulled me into her arms and hugged me tightly. I could hear the fast beating of her heart through her chest.

"Remember to be a good girl. Everything will be okay. I promise."

"Okay. I'll remember." My voice came out as a whimper as I tried to stay strong and not cry again. I could tell my mom was very sad, so I didn't want her to see me cry anymore.

Thirty minutes later, after I had hugged her for a very long time, I was sitting in the backseat of a car with Aunt Betty and Uncle Tom. The moment I felt the car engine roar to life, tears fell down my cheeks. I looked out the window and saw my mom crying, too.

"No! Mommy!" I cried out as I pressed my hands and face up against the closed window.

"Be good, Chloe! I'll see you soon. I promise."

As I struggled to breathe through my sobs, I wondered if she would keep that promise.

Chapter Five

Summer 1992

Seven Years Old

I woke up when the car finally pulled up to the driveway of Aunt Betty and Uncle Tom's house. When I realized what had happened, I was immediately upset with myself. I had wanted to pay attention to the roads and try to remember how to get back to the apartment complex my mom and I lived in.

I needed to know how to get home just in case my mom needed me.

"Aunt Betty?"

Aunt Betty had just unbuckled her seatbelt when she turned back to look at me. "Yes, honey? We're here." Being my mom's older sister, she looked a lot older but had the same smile as my mom, which comforted me.

"Can you draw me a map to me and mommy's apartment?"

She kept the smile on her face, but I could see a worried expression in her eyes. "Honey, your mommy's not going to live there anymore, remember? She's going to be living with other people who are also sick, and she's going to stay there until she gets better."

"Oh." I did remember my mom telling me that, but I was hoping things had changed. "Can I call her?"

"Of course. Let's first get settled in, and we'll call her before dinner. Okay?"

I nodded. I really wanted to tell Aunt Betty that I wanted to talk to my mom now, but I knew I was supposed to listen and be good.

"Now, come on. Let's see your new room," she said with excitement. "We have a surprise for you."

"Really?" I looked at Aunt Betty with a new sense of hope. A surprise? Maybe it's Mommy! Maybe Mommy is playing a joke on me.

I grabbed Belle, who was sitting in the seat next to me, and got out of the car. It was sticky-hot outside but I felt a little happier to know there was a surprise in my room. I looked up at Aunt Betty and Uncle's Tom's house in awe. It was so much bigger than the apartment. They had three spaces for their cars in the garage, which was bigger than my entire apartment with my mom.

"How come you didn't park your car in the garage, Uncle Tom?"

Uncle Tom chuckled. "You're a very smart and observant kid, Chloe."

"Mommy says I like to ask a lot of questions, and she says sometimes it's rude to ask too many questions. I'm sorry if I was rude, Uncle Tom."

"You weren't being rude. Being curious is a good thing." He reassured me with a smile. "And to answer your question, since Charlie is in college now, we moved his things to the garage for now, and his old room is your new room."

"Oh." I remembered Charlie. He was a lot older than me and I never really talked to him much. But he wasn't mean to me, so I liked him. "Will Charlie be mad if I'm in his room when he comes home?"

"No," Uncle Tom said with an understanding smile. "I mentioned it to him already. He's going to stay in the guest room when he's home from college. But because you'll be staying here for a while, we wanted you to have the bigger room so you feel more comfortable."

"Come on, Chloe," called out Aunt Betty as she walked to the front door. "It's really hot out. Let's get inside. Uncle Tom will grab the rest of your things."

"Okay, Aunt Betty." I hugged Belle a little tighter and whispered, "We're going to be living here for a little bit while Mommy gets better, Belle. Don't be scared, okay? I'll be here to protect you." I kissed Belle on the forehead, the way my mom would kiss me when she wanted to make things better.

As I walked up the driveway, a boy popped his head out from the treehouse between Aunt Betty and Uncle Tom's house and the even larger house next door. We stared at each other for a moment. I wanted to ask about his treehouse because I'd never seen one before in real life. But before I could ask, he yelled down, "You look like Pippi Longstocking!"

His words stung, and it made me mad. "I do not, you big meanie!" I screamed up at him.

"Pippi Longstocking!" He flashed me a boyish grin and he pointed to the pigtails my mom had braided for me that morning before we'd said goodbye.

"And you're a big, fat meanie!" I screamed up at him again, but this time, I stuck my tongue out and made a face at him, too.

Then I turned away and ran into the house because I didn't want the boy to see me upset.

"Did you make a new friend out there?" Uncle Tom said with a smile as he walked toward the staircase leading up to the second floor.

"No," I immediately retorted and twisted my face in disgust. "He said I look like Pippi Longstocking."

Aunt Betty laughed. "Sounds like someone has a crush on you, Chloe."

"No. He's mean." I frowned and wondered if Aunt Betty and Uncle Tom had problems with their hearing. There was no way that boy liked me.

"Give the poor boy a chance," Uncle Tom continued with a chuckle. "Sometimes boys just have a hard time expressing their feelings."

He didn't seem to have any problems expressing his feelings to me, I wanted to counter, but I remembered what my mom said and I knew that a good girl didn't talk back to adults. So I kept my thoughts to myself as I walked up the stairs with Aunt Betty and her husband. But I knew they were wrong. That boy didn't like me and I didn't like the boy, either. He was mean. He was a bully. He would never be my friend.

Minutes later, all thoughts of that boy vanished, because when I walked into my new room, I saw the surprise Aunt Betty and Uncle Tom had for me.

My eyes grew wide with glee as I took the entire room in. "Is this really my room?" The room was almost as big as the whole apartment my mom and I had lived in. I couldn't believe that such a large room was going to be just for me.

"Is that a dollhouse?" I squealed as I ran over to the corner of the room near the bay window where a large dollhouse stood. It was so tall that I had to get on my tippy toes to be able to touch the top of the roof with my hands.

"We heard that Belle was going to be living with us, too." Aunt Betty walked over to me with a smile and helped me open the dollhouse so we could see the inside. "So we wanted to make sure that she felt at home as well."

I gasped when I saw the inside. It wasn't a dollhouse; it was a doll-mansion. "Thank you, thank you, thank you, Aunt Betty! Belle's never had such a big house to herself." Then I cried out in delight and pointed at one of the rooms. "Look, Belle! There's a library in your house! Look at all those books you can read."

"So does that mean you like your room?" Aunt Betty's eyes twinkled as she smiled at me.

I nodded excitedly. "Thank you, Aunt Betty! Thank you, Uncle Tom!"

Uncle Tom flashed me a huge smile. "I don't think you've noticed the surprise."

"What do you mean?" I stared at him in confusion. "Isn't this room the surprise?"

Aunt Betty and Uncle Tom exchanged a look, like they knew a secret.

"Is Mommy here?" My eyes lit up in excitement as I looked around the room for places she could be hiding.

But then I noticed Aunt Betty and Uncle Tom exchange a look that made them seem worried. "Well …" Aunt Betty looked at me apologetically. "No, honey, your mommy isn't here." She then smiled, trying to convince me to do the same with her expectant eyes.

I felt downcast that my mom wasn't with me. I also felt guilty that a part of me felt excited about living in this big room when I didn't know where my mom would be living.

"The surprise is on the ceiling," she finally told me.

I immediately looked up to see what she was talking about. A loud gasp left my lips as I clutched Belle tighter with excitement. "Stars!" The entire grayish-blue ceiling of my room was covered with hundreds of stars of various sizes. "Is it the constellation?" My eyes lit up as I looked at Aunt Betty and then Uncle Tom for confirmation.

Uncle Tom nodded with a grin. "You're a smart girl, Chloe. Yes, it's the constellation."

"We heard you really love looking up at the sky at night and reading about things that occur in the sky," Aunt Betty explained. "Now you can sleep under all the stars."

I nodded with a smile as I looked up at all the stars.

"And guess what?" Uncle Tom asked.

"What?" My eyes went wide as I looked up at him.

"At night, all the stars will glow in the dark."

"They will?" I wasn't sure how that was possible, but I couldn't wait until it got dark. I had so much excitement coursing through me, it felt like I was on a sugar high after a night of trick-or-treating on Halloween. For the first time that day, I started to feel happy about being there.

Chapter Six

Summer 1992

Seven Years Old

"Okay, class," a tall lady with strawberry-blond hair in front of me called out from the front of the class to the other kids in the classroom, "it's time to get started. Everyone, take your seats." She turned and flashed me a warm smile. "I'm going to introduce you to everyone. Is that okay?"

I nodded. I sneaked a quick glance to all the kids sitting at their desks, who were now all staring at me with interest. My face felt hot and I looked down to my feet.

"Good morning, class."

"Good morning, Ms. Peters," the class greeted back in unison.

"Before we get started, I want everyone to say hello to Chloe Sinclair."

"Hello, Chloe Sinclair," the class repeated.

"Hi," I replied in a hesitant voice as I waved to everyone.

Ms. Peters smiled down at me. "Chloe just moved into the area and will be joining our first-grade class this year. Because she's new here, she is still figuring her way around the school. So if you see her around, please make sure she feels welcomed and answer any questions she may have, okay?"

"Yes, Ms. Peters," the class responded.

"Chloe, we're all really excited to get to know you. There's an empty desk in the third row. Why don't you take that one?"

"Okay. Thanks, Ms. Peters." I flashed her a smile before walking to the seat she pointed out.

As I walked up the row to my seat, a girl with pretty blond hair smiled at me. I smiled back and was about to say hi to her, but as I got closer to her, I noticed that her smile was more of a smirk.

"There are black holes on your overalls."

Feeling embarrassed, I looked down to inspect my red overalls and Strawberry Shortcake top. I noticed the small black burn marks the girl was talking about. They were from my mom's cigarettes. She would sometimes get clumsy when doing the laundry after she had some alcohol.

I didn't know what to say to the pretty girl, so I just walked past her and sat down at my seat.

"Okay, let's start out the day with some vocabulary," Ms. Peters called out from the front of the room and instructed us to take out our notebooks.

As I pulled the new notebook Aunt Betty had gotten me the other day from my backpack, I thought I heard someone whisper, "Pst! Hey."

I looked to my left and then my right and didn't see anyone looking at me.

But then the low whisper came again. "Pst! Pippi Longstocking."

My body froze when I heard those words. *It can't be him. Can it?* I finally looked around again, and there he was, in the next row, a desk back from mine. It was the boy I had seen in the treehouse a week ago, the mean boy who I wasn't going to be friends with.

"It's me," he whispered with his boyish grin.

"Duh," I shot back. I then stuck my tongue out at him and turned back around. I wasn't going to talk to him.

And I didn't. For that entire morning, he had tried to get my attention three more times, but I pretended that I couldn't hear him and looked straight ahead to the front of the class.

***

When lunchtime came, I started to feel nervous. In my old school, I used to sit at a small table with another girl who didn't seem to have any friends either. She was very shy and didn't talk much. But that was okay. I liked sitting next to her because she wasn't mean and didn't bother me.

I took my new Barbie lunchbox out of my backpack and looked for a place to sit and eat. The cafeteria was noisy, and smelled like tuna fish and French fries. As I walked around the large, crowded cafeteria, I couldn't see an empty table anywhere.

I was about to give up and go find an empty bench in the hallway, when to my delight, I heard someone say, "Hi, Chloe."

I quickly turned toward the voice and smiled. It was the pretty blond girl from my class.

"Hi … I don't know your name," I admitted sheepishly.

"It's Amber."

"Hi, Amber." I smiled and waved at her and the three other girls at the table. They giggled and said hi back.

"Where are you going to eat your lunch?" Amber asked.

"I don't know," I replied. I looked down at my feet and wished I was like her and had friends to sit with.

"Well, we have an extra seat here that you can sit in," she began and she pointed to the empty seat next to her.

My eyes lit up and I looked up at her as I felt the relief wash over me. "Really?" I asked hopefully and took a step toward her table.

"*But*," she continued and the same smirk from that morning spread across her face, "I don't think you want to sit with us."

I frowned. "What do you mean?"

"You're dirty and you love to sit on the ground so your clothes can get more dirt and black holes on them." She started to laugh and her friends joined in.

When I heard her words, I felt my face grow hot with embarrassment as tears welled up in my eyes. Aunt Betty had bought me some new clothes last week, but I wanted to wear my Strawberry Shortcake top and cherry-red overalls. They reminded me of my mom because it was her favorite. My mom had bought the top and overalls at a yard sale a year ago for only $0.50. I still remember how happy she was that it had fit me perfectly. She'd said it was her favorite because I'd looked as sweet as strawberries in the outfit.

"I'm not dirty," I finally said. I wanted to sound louder, but my words came out as a whisper. But I didn't wait to see if she had heard me. I turned around and began to run to the nearest exit to get away from their giggles.

But I only got past one table before I tripped over someone's extended foot. I watched in horror as my Barbie lunchbox flew out of my hand as I fell forward and landed across my chest.

"Oh my God, she totally ate it," Amber cried out as she called attention to my fall.

An explosion of laughter echoed in the cafeteria as my chest started to hurt from the impact. I could feel everyone's eyes on me as I remained face down on the green-and-white checkered vinyl floor. I didn't want to get up. Not because my body hurt, but because I didn't want everyone to see me cry.

Then I heard someone walk up to me. I held my breath and prepared myself for more embarrassment.

"Amber's breath smells like stinky farts," cried out a boy's voice. "Don't let her breathe on you!" Another uproar of laughter exploded around me, but to my relief, it didn't seem to be directed at me.

I turned my head slightly and tried to see who was making fun of Amber. But before I could see who it was, Amber screamed in a piercing voice, "It does not! You take that back, Jackson!"

Jackson just laughed. "But it's the truth," he continued with mirth in his voice. "That's why you chew gum all the time when we're not allowed to."

"That's not true at all!" Amber screamed. I couldn't see her but it sounded like she was about to cry. Just as I picked my head up to look in her direction, I saw Amber storm past me and in the direction of the cafeteria door. "I hate you, Jackson Pierce! I'm going to tell your mom."

"That's because you're a tattletale! Tattletale Amber." The boy named Jackson laughed, and to my surprise, several kids started laughing and chanting, "Tattletale Amber. Tattletale Amber."

A part of me felt bad that everyone was laughing at Amber for having stinky breath and being a tattletale, but I was more relieved that no one seemed to be looking at me anymore.

"Hey, take my hand," came Jackson's voice from behind me.

I smiled and wanted to hug this boy who had helped me. But when I turned around and rolled to my back to face him, I gasped.

The boy named Jackson—the boy who had just saved me from evil Tattletale Amber—was the same boy in the treehouse who lived next door, the same boy who called me Pippi Longstocking the first time we met, the same boy whom I hated.

"It's you," I blurted out as I stared at him and his outstretched hand.

"Yes, last time I checked, I am me." He smirked, probably proud of himself for being such a smart-ass. "Come on, take my hand." He held out his hand to me and smiled down at me.

I didn't want his help, not from a boy who had been mean to me. But then I remembered what he had just done for me. He had been mean to Amber so people would stop laughing at me. *But can I trust him?* I wondered, hesitant to let my guard down with this boy.

But when I met his gaze, I felt myself relax. There was a warmth in his eyes that was echoed in his smile, and my hand reached up for his before I realized it. As his hand clasped firmly around mine, I felt safe and comforted.

"Thank you," I said softly as he pulled me up from the ground. Then he handed me my lunchbox. "Oh." I looked at it in surprise. "Thanks for picking that up too."

"No problem." He brushed off some dust from the front of my overalls. "Amber isn't very nice. You should be careful with her."

I nodded, realizing I learned it the hard way that Amber was not nice. "But why did you help me, then? You weren't careful with her. What if she does something to you?" All of a sudden, I was worried for Jackson. Even though he hadn't been nice to me before, I didn't want Amber to be mean to him because he had helped me.

Jackson grinned, his green eyes sparkling in the light. "She won't," he said confidently.

"Why not?"

"Because she has a crush on me." He shook his body like he was shuddering and scrunched his face to look disgusted.

"Really? She does?" I looked at Jackson and wondered if it was true. I could see how some girls might think he was cute, with his pretty, green eyes and tousled warm-chestnut hair. But I didn't like boys. My mom always told me they will only make girls cry, and I didn't like to cry.

"You can eat at my table, if you'd like."

"I can?" I looked at him eagerly. "You don't think I'm dirty?"

"Nah. Kids are supposed to be a little dirty. If you're not dirty, you're boring."

I giggled and liked his reasoning. *Maybe he's not so mean after all,* I thought.

When we got to his table, the two other boys said hi to me quickly before going back to their conversation about yesterday's episode of *Batman.*

"Do you watch cartoons?" Jackson asked me.

"A little," I said noncommittally.

"What superhero would you be if you could choose?"

I stared at him and giggled. *Is this what boys talked about?* "I don't know. Who would you be?"

"I'd be Michelangelo!" He got up from his seat, clenched his fists and made a karate move in front of me. "He's funny and loves pizza the most. I love pizza!"

"Okay." I tried not to giggle at how excited he was.

"I know everything about the *Ninja Turtles*. It's my favorite show." He sat back down next to me. "Since you don't know who you'd be, you can be April O'Neil."

"Why?"

"Because the Ninja Turtles saved her life, like I saved you earlier."

I rolled my eyes. "The Ninja Turtles are just large turtles who got lucky and had Master Splinter train them."

His eyes lit up and he leaned toward me. "So you do watch the show."

"I don't," I denied, even though secretly, it was one of my favorite shows.

"You wanna come over and play after school? We can watch it together?" He seemed to have ignored me completely.

I stared at him and tried to remind myself that he had made fun of me last week.

"Why would you want me to watch it with you?" I looked at him dubiously.

"Because we're friends, silly." He rolled his eyes. "Duh!"

"Friends?" I tilted my head and looked over at him, wondering if I heard him correctly.

"Yeah. Why?" He frowned. "You don't wanna be my friend?"

I shrugged. "I've never had a friend before."

"Never?" He looked at me in surprise.

I bowed my head and shook it slowly, feeling embarrassed about this. "There weren't any kids where I lived."

"Oh." He paused. "Well, that means, I'll be your first friend!"

I couldn't help but smile at what he said.

"So, *Ninja Turtles* after school, then?"

I smiled, feeling happy that I'd met a new friend—my very first friend.

Chapter Seven

November 1994

Nine Years Old

"I seriously love your aunt." Jackson licked his spoon, savoring the last traces of the chicken pot pie I'd brought over.

I shook my head in amazement, looking from Jackson's empty plate to my barely-eaten pot pie. "You know, if I didn't know you lived in a huge house like this, with a fridge stocked full of food, I'd think you hadn't eaten a decent meal in weeks."

He laughed. "Well, you're just spoiled and don't understand how delicious your aunt's cooking is."

"Yeah, you're probably right." I only had to look around at Jackson's house to know what he'd meant. While his house was almost twice the size of mine, it didn't nearly feel as comfortable. Besides Jackson's room, every other room of the house looked like they'd come straight out of some interior design magazine. Everything looked expensive and immaculate, but felt cold and not lived in.

"Coaster," Jackson warned as he watched me almost place my glass of water on the bare maple dining table.

"Oh, oops." I flashed him an apologetic smile. "Sorry, I always forget."

Jackson relaxed a little. "It's okay. My mom's just a little picky about everything."

"Yeah, I know." I looked around. "Everything's spotless."

He shrugged. "Like it matters. It's not like they're home much to even enjoy it."

I frowned and placed a hand on his shoulder. "Your parents work really hard to take care of you. I'm sure if they had a choice, they'd much rather be home than be stuck at work all the time."

He sighed. "Yeah, you're right. I just wish we had regular family dinners like you guys, and not once every week or so."

"Aunt Betty and Uncle Tom are great," I admitted, "but I would give almost anything to be able to have weekly dinners with my mom and dad," I said wistfully.

"Crap. Sorry, Chloe. I shouldn't be so insensitive sometimes when I complain about my parents."

I flashed him a reassuring smile. "It's okay. You're not being insensitive. You shouldn't feel bad for wishing your parents were more around for you."

"Yeah, but I feel like such a jerk when I do. Your dad died before you were born and you don't get to see your mom that often—"

"It's okay," I said, cutting him off. I didn't really want to be reminded of what I didn't have. "Let's talk about something else." I tried to sound cheerful as I forced a smile on my face.

Just then we heard the door to the garage open down the hall.

"Jackson? You home?" a voice called out.

"Hey, Dad. In the dining room," Jackson called out.

"Well, look who's here," Mr. Pierce said with a smile as he walked through the entrance the kitchen.

"Hi, Mr. Pierce." I returned his smile.

"Now, now. Call me John, Chloe. 'Mr. Pierce' makes me sound old." He chuckled.

But you are old, I thought to myself, but would never dare to say out loud. I forced a small laugh. "Ok…John."

"Much better." He then turned to Jackson. "Sorry, my office hours ran a bit late this afternoon. Finals are coming up, so I've been getting a line of students with last minute questions. Did Maria leave already?"

"Yeah, she left about an hour ago. She said your dry cleaning is in your closet."

"Okay, great." He looked at his watch. "Did she order you dinner?"

"No, Chloe's aunt sent over some chicken pot pie, so I told Maria not to order me anything for dinner." Maria was the person Jackson's parents had hired to look after him when they weren't home.

"That's so nice of her." He then turned to look at me and smiled. "Please tell your aunt 'thank you' for me, Chloe."

"Sure thing."

As Mr. Pierce walked past us, he put a hand on my shoulder and squeezed it. "Thanks for taking care of my son. I don't know what he'd do without you."

I blushed.

"Dad, stop it. You're embarrassing me," Jackson complained as he got up from his chair. "We got to get going. We're going over to hang out at the park for a bit."

Mr. Pierced laughed as he walked over to the fridge and took out a bottle of water. "You know, Chloe," he began, looking backed at me, "it takes a special girl like you to make Jackson embarrassed and flustered. Don't break his heart." He then winked at me before taking a swig from his water bottle.

Feeling a bit uncomfortable with his comment, I quickly explained, "We're just friends, Mr. Pierce."

"John," he corrected.

"Right. Sorry. John. We're just good friends."

"Good to know." He looked between us. "Well, I'm heading up to my office. I still have some papers to grade."

"Good night, Mr.—I mean, John."

"Have a nice night, guys. Don't stay out too late."

"We won't, Dad. See yah."

It took me and Jackson fifteen minutes to walk to the park from the house. Besides Jackson's treehouse, the small lake at the center of the park was one of our favorite places to hang out. It was a cold night and the park was showing its beginning signs of winter. But after our walk, the cold air felt nice against my face. The sun had just disappeared beyond the horizon and we were lying on the grass next to the lake, staring up at the sky and watching the stars begin to appear.

"It's beautiful, isn't it?" I let out a deep sigh as my eyes took in the wide expanse of the twilight-colored sky, marveling at how beautiful something so simple could be.

"Yeah, it's pretty cool." I could tell from his tone that he was unimpressed and was only here because I had wanted to come.

"Jax?" I turned to face Jackson, calling him by my nickname for him. He turned his head to face me. "Yeah, Clo?" he replied with his nickname for me. I heard him picking at the grass underneath his hands.

"What do you want to be when you grow up?"

"Hmm. I don't know. I'm only ten."

"Come on," I insisted. "If you could be anything you wanted, what would it be?"

He stared at the sky in silence for a few seconds. Then from the corner of my eye, I saw a smirk appear on his face.

"What?" I asked suspiciously.

"I know what I want to be."

"Okay. What?" I was feeling a bit impatient.

He turned back to look at me and grinned. "A kid." He laughed at his own joke and then he threw a handful of grass on my face.

"Hey!" I spat out a few pieces of grass that had landed in my mouth. "Why did you have to do that?" I screeched, feeling a mixture of annoyance and delight as I ripped up a handful of grass and threw it back at him.

"Because it's fun." He laughed as he rolled away from me, avoiding the pieces of grass and dirt that landed in front of him. I tried to chase him down, but he kept his distance, dodging my every attempt to grab him.

After a few minutes of the unsuccessful cat-and-mouse chase, I finally had to stop to catch my breath. We stared at each other, both laughing and panting.

"You're way too fast for me." I shook my head, annoyed that not only had he gotten a bit faster than me in the past few years, he'd also grown a few inches taller and stronger.

"That's because I have superhero powers!" He put his fisted hands on his hips and looked up to his right, mimicking a Superman stance.

I rolled my eyes. "You wish. It's only because you're a boy and you grow faster than me. Aunt Betty said that's normal."

"You're just saying that because you're jealous you don't have my superhero speed and can't catch up to me."

"No, I'm not jealous." I pouted. "I just don't know why you had to throw grass in my mouth. I thought we're friends." I huffed and turned away from him, making sure he knew I was mad at him—even though I really wasn't.

"Come on, don't be like that," he cajoled.

"Be like what?" I turned to him. "I don't know about you, but I don't really like to eat grass."

"Well, I didn't see you eat any, if that helps." He flashed me one of his innocent-but-not-so-innocent smiles. "Besides, I'm *only* trying to answer your question."

I frowned, completely forgetting what I had asked him. "And what question was that?"

"What I wanted to be when I grew up." His face struggled to keep the laughter at bay.

"You want to throw grass into people's faces when you grow up?" I challenged, knowing he was trying to be a smart-ass.

"No," he countered, "just yours." He then bent down, grabbed another fist full of grass, and aimed it at me. But this time, I was ready for him and turned away just in time.

"Well, I hope you enjoy being a kid all your life. That sounds so boring to have to go to school forever," I teased him.

"But I'd be the smartest kid in my class," he retorted. "That sounds pretty cool."

I rolled my eyes, but couldn't help giggling when I pictured an old, adult Jackson sitting in the small school desks with other fourth graders.

"Why do you wanna know that, anyway?" he asked, sounding more serious as he sat back down on the grass. "You know it's going to, like, take *forever* before we grow up."

I smiled at his comment and sat next to him. I envied Jax. In many ways, his life seemed so simple and carefree compared to mine. I liked that he always had a way of reminding me that I was still just a kid.

"Well, I'm turning ten next week, and I've been thinking a lot about the future."

"Oh. So what do you want to be when you grow up?"

"I want a job where I can travel to all parts of the world." I smiled at the thought.

"You do?" He looked at me and I could tell that wasn't what he'd expected me to say and it wasn't something he'd ever thought about.

"Yeah, I think it would be amazing. There are so many places in the world I want to see, but have only read about in the *Reader's Digest* and *Discover* magazines that Uncle Tom gets me every year."

"Really?" His face twisted into a frown. "I don't know much about that stuff." He paused, thinking to himself. "So what's one place in the world you'd want to go to the most?"

I looked out across the lake and thought about it. "If I had to pick only one, the one thing I want to see most is an aurora borealis."

"A roar-what?"

I giggled. "An aurora borealis. Some people call it the Northern Lights."

"What is that?" He looked at me with interest.

"I've only seen pictures but it looks magical. It's a natural phenomenon that happens in the sky in places that are in high altitudes. I don't really understand the science behind it, but I have tried to read a lot about it. An aurora borealis occurs at night, and when it happens, the sky is suddenly lit up and filled with bright reds, greens, yellows, and blues across the sky, and they're swirling around like they're dancing in a lava lamp. It sounds so cool to me."

"That does sound really cool." Jackson looked up into the sky. "So where do you go to see an aurora—the Northern Lights?"

"Aurora borealis. I think there're a lot of places you can go, like Canada, Alaska, Norway, and Iceland. But the place that I saw in a magazine that looked so cool was this town called Kakslauttanen, Finland."

"Ka-what?" Jackson stared at me in confusion. "How do you even remember these names or know how to pronounce it?"

I grinned, knowing how much of a nerd I must have sounded to him. "I kept that page of the magazine and have it in my desk in my room. I look at it sometimes when I want to daydream."

"Oh. So what's so special about this Kaka-whatever place?"

"Well, from the article I saw, they have a resort there where you stay in these private room-size glass igloos in the middle of a national park, and you can look out from anywhere in your room and watch the Northern Lights overhead as they swirl around all night." I let out a wistful sigh. "It just sounds so amazing, doesn't it?"

"Yeah, that really sounds cool."

For several minutes, we sat there next to each other in silence as we looked out onto the lake, enjoying each other's company without saying a word—it was a level of comfort that I only felt with him.

Then I felt a pang of guilt as I thought about my mom. "I also want to be able to take care of my mom when I grow up."

"You will," he assured me with a smile. He turned and met my gaze. Even though it was dark, his emerald eyes seemed to twinkle as he looked at me. Like his smile, they were warm, inviting, genuine. They always seemed to be able to comfort me when I needed it.

"Thanks." I tried to return his smile.

"So how is she lately?"

I shrugged. It wasn't something Jackson and I talked about very often—mostly because it wasn't something I wanted to talk about very often. I missed her and wished things were different, but no matter what I did, I always seemed to feel guilty where she was involved. I felt guilty when I thought about her because I was just reminded that I wasn't there for her when she was sick. I felt guilty when I tried not to think of her, too, because I felt like a bad daughter for trying to enjoy my life without her.

"She's about the same," I finally said. "Aunt Betty says she has rebounds, so she's been in and out of the places that are supposed to help her."

"Oh." I could tell Jackson was uncomfortable when we talked about my mom because I was always sad when we talked about her.

"Aunt Betty said that my mom had to go back to different places to try to get better. And that was why I can't live with her. The people who made me live with Aunt Betty and Uncle Tom won't let me move back with my mom until she's able to get completely better."

"I see." Jax looked at me and then looked away. I could tell he wanted to say something but didn't want to hurt my feelings. He made that same face when I would bring him a lunchbox item that he didn't really want to eat but didn't want to hurt my feelings by telling me. Sometimes he'd eat it anyway to make me happy. Other times, I'd seen him try to throw it away when he didn't think I was watching.

"What are you thinking?" I finally asked.

"Nothing," he said quickly.

"No, tell me. Come on." I pushed out my lips in a pout. "I'm not going to get mad, I promise."

He looked at me before asking, "Okay, you promise?"

I nodded.

"Well…" He paused. "I like that you don't live with your mom, and you live with your aunt and uncle."

I felt a little hurt by his words. "Why would you want my mom to be sick?"

"No," he said quickly and shook his head. "I don't want your mom to be sick. I … I just like that you live next door, and not far away from me." He bowed his head and began to shift uncomfortably. "I would really miss you."

"Oh." The hurt I felt moments ago was gone, and a warm feeling across my chest took its place. "I would miss you too, Jax."

"You would?" His whole face lit up as he met my gaze.

I smiled. "Yeah. Of course. You're my first and best friend. I would miss hanging out with you."

"Best friend?" He smiled, but the gleam in his eyes wasn't there anymore.

"Yes. Best friends forever." I beamed at him, feeling so lucky to be able to share my secrets with him.

***

November 1994

Ten Years Old

A pair of hands grabbed me from behind, causing me to shriek and drop the pristine *Charlotte's Web* book in my hands.

"Happy birthday!" Jax jumped up in front of me with a big grin on his face.

"Thanks," I said absentmindedly as I quickly bent down to pick up the book. I brushed off some dust and examined it to make sure the corners were not damaged. I let out a sigh of relief; it was still perfect.

"What's that?" He eyed the brand new book in my hand.

"It's a birthday gift from my mom." I ran my hand across the cover and smiled. "It's a first edition copy of *Charlotte's Web*, my favorite book."

"Oh really? I thought you hadn't seen her in a while."

The truth of his words stung.

"Aunt Betty gave it to me this morning before school."

"Oh." He scrunched his face. "How do you know it's from your mom, then?"

"Aunt Betty said so."

"Oh." He didn't say another word, but I knew what he was thinking.

I was thinking the same thing. Did my mom really get me a present? Did she even remember my birthday? Or was this gift really from Aunt Betty and Uncle Tom?

"That's a nice gift," Jackson said in a rush of excitement, quickly changing his tune when he noticed the frown on my face. "You love to read so your mom must have really been thinking of you."

"Yeah." I flashed him a smile, but a part of me felt sad. I looked back at the book in my hand, and the cover looked a little less glossy and pretty than it had a minute ago. I realized then that I'd never mentioned *Charlotte's Web* to my mom before during any of my visits.

"Here's your lunch." I pulled a brown paper bag from my opened locker and handed it to Jackson, trying to change the subject.

"Oh. What did Aunt Betty pack today?" Jackson grabbed the bag from my hand and dug into it without waiting another minute.

I shrugged and followed him toward our next class together. "I think she made that roast beef panini you really like."

"God, she's the best!" His eyes lit up like it was Christmas. For as long as I'd known Jackson, his parents weren't home very much. His dad was a professor at University of Pennsylvania and his mom was a corporate attorney at some big law firm in

Philadelphia. They both worked long hours and always gave Jackson money for lunch. But Jackson had gotten sick of school cafeteria food years ago and I had started giving him half of the lunch Aunt Betty would make me. When Aunt Betty discovered this, she started to make two lunches every morning so that there would always be enough for the both of us.

"So wha does da buffday girl want to do today?" Jackson asked with a mouthful of the roast beef sandwich.

I laughed. "Jax. It's only ten thirty in the morning. We still have two more periods left before lunch."

"What? I'm hungry?" He shrugged and took another large bite of the sandwich.

I shook my head. "Just don't eat half of my lunch when it's actually lunchtime because you've finished yours."

He gave me a sheepish smile. "Well, no promises there."

I giggled and punched him playfully on the arm.

"So seriously, though, what would you like to do today after school?"

I frowned, feeling a heaviness in my heart. "I'd *like* to see my mom today for my tenth birthday; I'd *like* my mom to smile and hum to me while she braids my hair." I paused, realizing how bitter I sounded. "Never mind. I don't have any plans." I walked a little faster ahead so he couldn't see the moisture in my eyes.

"Wait—" He ran after me. "It's your birthday. Why can't you do that? I can see if Maria can take us if your aunt and uncle can't get out of work to take you."

I couldn't help but smile at Jackson's offer. "Thanks … but that's okay. Aunt Betty said that it's not a good idea to visit her right now."

"What? Why not?"

"She says my mom's been really sick and her doctor doesn't think I should see her at this time."

"Oh."

I watched Jackson put the rest of his sandwich back into the paper bag. "That sucks, Clo. I'm sorry." He grabbed my hand and pulled me in for a hug.

I was going to resist, and had for just a second, but as soon as he wrapped his arms around me, I knew that it was exactly what I needed at that moment.

Chapter Eight

Spring 1998

Thirteen Years Old

It was the call no one is ever prepared for. It was the call no one ever wants to receive. It was the call no one ever wishes upon even their worst enemies.

But it was the call I was about to receive that day.

It was an idle Wednesday afternoon, much like any other during a school week. I was at home doing my homework and waiting for Jackson to come over after he was done with his track practice.

I was working on my pre-algebra problem, sitting at the coffee table in the living room while MTV's *Total Request Live* was playing in the background. Carson Daly was talking to a few people from the live studio audience at the moment but I knew he was about to reveal the sixth most requested music video of the day. I had my fingers crossed that it would be Savage Garden's "Truly Madly Deeply," my favorite song. I'd been calling and voting every day for several months now to make sure it was getting enough votes. I'd even had Jackson call and vote from the phone in his house every day—okay, so most days I'd had to call for him, but to me, that was merely a technicality, and at the end of the day, "Truly Madly Deeply" was getting at least two votes every day. It was number six yesterday and being the loyal fan that I was, I didn't want it to fall to seventh place. So I was anxiously waiting for Carson to announce the video that was in sixth place.

Just then, the telephone started to ring. I walked over to the kitchen counter to grab the phone, my eyes never leaving the TV screen.

"…and number six on TRL today is…" Carson started to say. I held my breath as I picked up the phone to answer it.

"Hello," I said absentmindedly into the receiver, my focus still on Carson.

"… "Truly Madly Deeply" by Savage Garden!"

"Woo!" I cheered out loud as the music video started on the screen.

"Chloe?" I heard Aunt Betty's voice calling out to me.

"Hey, Aunt Betty. Sorry about that. My favorite song just came on." My body started swaying with the beat of the song.

"That's nice, honey," she said in an eerily soft voice. "Um, so I wanted to let you know that I'm on my way home right now." There was a rawness in her voice that gave me pause and I immediately felt my entire body tense up.

"What is it? Is something wrong, Aunt Betty?"

"I'll be home soon." I noticed she didn't answer my question.

I felt a wave of panic prickle down my body. "Are you okay? Are you hurt? Is Uncle Tom okay?" I asked her in quick bursts of alarm.

"Y—yes, we're both fine. We're not hurt." Her words stumbled out and I could tell she was flustered and anxious about something.

"What's wrong?" I looked at the clock and realized Jackson hadn't shown up yet. "Is it Jackson? Please don't tell me it's Jackson, Aunt Betty." I felt my chest tighten with worry as the thought of something happening to Jackson tore at my insides.

"No, honey. Please calm down. It's not Jackson." Her voice was overly soothing and strangely disconcerting, inducing the opposite effect she'd probably intended.

"What is it, then? What are you not telling me?"

"I just exited the freeway, so I'll be home soon. We can talk then."

I searched anxiously for the meaning behind her words, trying to piece together a logical explanation for her odd behavior. It was clear she had something to tell me, but she didn't want to say it over the phone. *She says she's okay, Uncle Tom's okay, and Jackson's okay ... so what else can it be?*

Then, as if clarity had smacked me against the face, another person came to mind. Suddenly, a wave of apprehension swept through me.

"Is it my mom?" I cried out, my voice rising an octave higher.

There was a brief silence before she answered, and yet it felt like a lifetime.

"Honey, I'll be home in less than two minutes," she insisted. "Just wait for me, okay?"

My stomach twisted in agony, knowing her response was no different than saying "yes." Something had happened to my mom and it must not be good news if Aunt Betty wanted to tell me in person.

As the overwhelming flood of fear and anxiety began to consume my thoughts, I tried to think back to the last time I'd seen my mom. It'd been almost a month ago when I had visited her at the long-term rehabilitation facility she was staying at. She was nearing the end of her three-month stay, and she looked healthy, sober, and happy. I had updated her on everything that'd been going on with me since the previous time I'd seen her. She had promised me that after she left the rehab facility, she wouldn't need to return to one again. She had promised me that she felt like she wasn't sick anymore. She had promised me that I'd be able to move back in with her soon.

"Chloe?" came a voice from behind me. "Chloe?"

I turned to the voice. It was Aunt Betty standing at the opening of the kitchen area and looking at me with concern in her blood-shot eyes.

"Are you okay, honey? I called out your name several times before you turned around."

Her blood-shot eyes! As if someone had just flipped a switch inside me, I leaped to Aunt Betty's side. "Is my mom okay?"

The moment I saw her face twist in agony, I knew I didn't want to hear it.

"Honey," she began slowly, "I think you need to sit down for this."

I sat down quickly to appease her before blurting out, "Where's my mom right now?" I searched her face for answers, growing more impatient by the second.

"Chloe … there's no easy way to say this, and you're old enough where I need to just be straight forward with you."

"Did she have another rebound? Where is she now?" Panic tightened its vicious grip on me as I tried to hang on to the possibility that it wasn't what I feared the most.

But, like many times before, I was wrong.

"Chloe, your mom passed away this morning." Her voice was shaky, but the words came out as clear as day.

Even though I heard her, I just stared at her, unable to process what she'd said. I felt numb and didn't know how to react to her words.

"They found her in her apartment this morning when she hadn't checked in with her sponsor like she was supposed to." She paused as she wiped the tears from her face. "They said she overdosed on some over-the-counter—" Aunt Betty's words broke off mid-sentence.

She threw her arms around me and began to sob uncontrollably. "I'm so sorry, Chloe. I know how much you wanted her to get better."

I stood there, unable to move, and watched Aunt Betty weep for her younger sister. I knew I should feel intense pain. I knew I should be sobbing for my loss. I knew I should be reacting to this news about the woman I'd loved the most in this life.

But I felt nothing.

"Chloe?" Aunt Betty finally noticed that something was wrong with me, that I hadn't made a single sound since she'd broken the news. "Are you okay, honey?"

"I'm fine." That was the only response I knew how to give. That was how I felt. Fine.

I couldn't seem to feel the pain. I couldn't seem to shed a tear. I couldn't seem to react at all. The only thing I seemed to be able to feel was the all-consuming numbness that seemed to shield me from the rest of the world.

***

My mom's funeral was held a week after she'd passed. It was very much like her life: dark, meager, short-lived, and attended by just a few.

It was a simple ceremony that lasted no more than fifteen minutes from start to finish. In addition to the dense layers of dark, threatening clouds overhead, only Aunt Betty, Uncle Tom, Jackson, Jackson's father, my mom's sponsor, and I were in attendance.

After the casket was lowered into the ground and we'd each thrown our handful of dirt onto the casket, people started to say their goodbyes as the small group started to head back to their cars.

I purposely lingered behind everyone, wanting to spend a few more minutes in front of the casket alone with her.

The idea that she was gone, that I would never see her again, that I would never hear her voice again, was something that hadn't sunk in. It was something my head hadn't wrapped itself around. It was something my heart hadn't accepted. It was something my body hadn't felt.

"You promised, Mom," I whispered as I stood over the open grave. "Why did you have to leave me? Did you do it on purpose? Was I not worth living for? You promised you'd get better and I'd move in with you soon. You promised…"

"Hey, Chloe," came a voice from behind me.

I turned and saw that it was Jackson's dad walking over from where the rest of the group stood talking.

"Hi, John." After the years of correcting me, I'd finally gotten used to calling Jackson's dad by his first name.

"I'm really sorry for your loss."

I just nodded, not quite sure what else to say. I couldn't tell him that I hadn't shed a single tear since my mom died, that I hadn't felt any sadness or anger, that I felt absolutely nothing.

"I can't imagine what you must be going through right now."

"Yeah."

"Jackson mentioned that you didn't get a chance to see her too often."

I frowned. I wasn't interested in talking about my mom, but I didn't think there was a polite way to say that.

"You're a good kid, Chloe. Even when you first moved in with your aunt and uncle, you were a good kid. I remember thinking what a good influence you were on Jackson, and how much he matured over the years."

"Oh. Thanks." I was surprised by the depth of this conversation. They were more words than we'd ever shared before.

"Do you know what that means, though?" He waited for me to respond.

"What?" I asked tentatively.

"It means that your mom raised you well, and your aunt and uncle continued raising you well. But it's important to remember that it started with your mom. I can tell that your mom loved you very much and cared about you."

"Sure." I wasn't convinced by his words. He didn't know anything about my mom. How would he know if she really cared about me or not?

As if sensing my doubt, he continued, "I know it might be hard to see, but as a parent, it's crystal clear to me. Maybe she didn't always know how to tell you that she loved you, but she showed it in how well she raised you."

His words made me think of all the hours my mom had spent teaching me how to think for myself and be responsible. Even when she felt sick from drinking too much the night before, she'd always made time for me and my endless questions.

"Thank you, John. I think you're right. My mom was a good mother." It was a revelation I hadn't expected to have.

He reached over and patted my shoulder. "I have no doubt that your mom must have been so proud of you."

"Thanks, John."

He smiled and nodded before leaving me standing alone in front of my mom's grave.

"Jackson's dad was right, Mom. You were an amazing mom. I wish I had thanked you for everything you've done for me. I know it couldn't have been easy to raise me alone." I paused and started to feel emotional. "Mom, I'll miss you so much."

Suddenly my legs gave out and I fell to my knees in front of her grave. Then, for the first time in my life, I let go of all the pain, anger, and resentment I'd ever buried inside for my mom. When I let go of all the negative feelings I'd kept inside, tears of pain and loss started streaming down my face as all the fond memories I had of my mom started flooding to the surface. It was as if the floodgates to my emotions opened, and all the tears I hadn't cried and all the pain that I hadn't felt came crashing down on me all at once. With every single tear and every ounce of pain, I was finally saying my goodbyes to the woman who loved me more than she'd loved herself.

Chapter Nine

Spring 1998

Thirteen Years Old

"Honey?" There was a soft knock at my bedroom door.

I glanced up from the TV but didn't respond.

"Honey?" Aunt Betty called out to me again. "I brought you some dinner."

"I'm not hungry," I finally said to the door that separated us.

"Honey, you haven't been eating all day. You need to try to eat something. You're going to get yourself sick if you starve yourself like this."

I knew she was right. I knew she only meant well. Feeling a little guilty for making her worried, I got up from my bed and walked over to open the door for her.

Her face brightened and I could almost see her body relax and let out a sigh with relief. "So I wasn't sure what you wanted to eat. You missed breakfast and lunch, but I made you your favorites so you can just eat whatever looks good to you."

In her hand was a large tray of food. There was a plate of bacon, hash browns, and sunny-side-up eggs, a bowl of macaroni and cheese, and a plate of her famous chicken pot pie.

"Thanks, Aunt Betty." I took the tray from her and set it down on my desk. "You really didn't have to go through all this trouble."

"No trouble at all, Chloe. I just want to make sure you're okay." I knew that was more of a question than a statement.

"Yeah. I'm okay. I'm just still trying to accept the fact that she's gone." I frowned.

She gave me an understanding smile. "I know, honey. I miss her, too. It was just very sudden and she looked like she had been doing great at our last visit, so there was no way we could've known."

"Aunt Betty?" There was something I'd been wanting to ask her ever since the funeral last week.

"What is it, Chloe?" Her familiar, kind face looked more sunken in and tired.

"Do you think she took all those painkillers on purpose?"

There was a brief silence as Aunt Betty's face turned somber. "I," —she let out a deep sigh— "I think it's a possibility."

I nodded, unable to respond in any other way at that moment. A part of me had thought that Aunt Betty would humor me and tell me my mom wouldn't have done such a thing, but instead, she told me what she really thought.

"Do you think if I'd seen her more often, she wouldn't have…" My voice cracked and I couldn't finish my question.

"Oh, honey. Please don't do this to yourself." She reached over and pulled me in for a hug. "This did not happen because of you. Your mom has been battling depression since before you were born. Some days she'd be fine, but other days she'd turn to alcohol and drugs to cope. And over the years, it just got worse and worse. There was nothing you could have done. This was her battle that she had to face alone. This was her demon that she'd been facing for a very long time."

"I just feel so guilty, though," I whispered, my words slightly muffled against her chest. "I just keep imagining how alone and sad she must have been to do such a thing, to give up like that, to feel like there was nothing left in this world to live for."

"Chloe, listen to me." She pulled me from her arms to look me in the eyes. "Your mother loved you, *very* much. You were the most important thing in her life. You have to understand that she probably wasn't thinking straight when she took those pills. She wasn't asking herself if there was anything to live for."

I knew she was right, but it didn't seem to matter. Knowing she loved me didn't bring her back. Aunt Betty stayed with me in my room for another half-hour, forcing me to eat at least five mouthfuls of food before she would leave my room. When she finally left me, I felt exhausted and lonely. I realized I didn't want to be by myself. I didn't want to spend any more time inside my head where I would just think about my mom and wonder what I could have done differently.

A part of me wanted to call out to Aunt Betty and ask her to stay with me for a bit longer. But then there was the other part of me that didn't want to admit that I needed any help.

But before I could make a decision on what to do, there was a soft knock at my door again.

"Chloe? It's me again," Aunt Betty's voice came from the other side of the door. "Jackson's here to see you. Do you want me to have him come up? Or do you want me to send him away?"

"He can come up. Thanks, Aunt Betty."

A few minutes later, Jackson walked in to my room. "Hey."

I could tell he was a little nervous. We hadn't seen each other since the funeral, and other than a few vacations he'd gone on with his parents, it'd been the longest period of time we'd been apart. It wasn't because he hadn't tried to see me. He had. But each time he'd stopped by to see me, I'd told Aunt Betty that I wasn't ready to see anyone.

"Hi. Thanks for coming to see me." It wasn't until I saw Jackson that I realized how much I'd missed him during the last several days.

He walked over slowly and sat down next to me on the bed. "How are you?"

I shrugged.

He nodded as if to say he understood.

There was a long moment of silence before he finally spoke again.

"So, I've been doing a lot of reading lately."

My ears perked up and I slowly looked at him. "Reading? But you don't really like to read, outside of mandatory school stuff." I tried to think back to all the times I'd seen him read or mention reading something outside of school-assigned reading in case I was wrong.

His lips curled into a small smile. "Yeah, I don't usually. But I wasn't sure what to do."

Understanding what he meant, I rolled my eyes. "Jax, you have other friends besides me to hang out with. And you love watching TV and browsing the internet—"

"No. No. You misunderstood me," he interrupted. "I meant I've been doing a lot of reading about…well…about what you're going through right now and how a friend is supposed to help."

"Oh." I was touched by his desire to understand what I was going through.

He looked down and looked uncomfortable. "Clo, it really kills me to see you so sad, and I just didn't know what I could do to help you."

I shook my head apologetically. "Jax, there isn't really anything you can do, just like there isn't really anything *I* can do."

"I know." He nodded solemnly. "All the things I've read said that it takes time, and what you need right now is time."

"Yeah."

"But I think you need something else as well."

"Oh? What's that?"

"You need me. You need to be around the people you care about and the people who care about you."

His words struck a chord with me, and I knew he was right. When Aunt Betty had left me alone earlier, I knew that was the last thing I had wanted.

But before I could agree with him, he continued. "I know you, and you don't want people to help you. You want to face this alone because you're so used to facing life's challenges on your own. So you never ask for help. But..." His voice cracked. Suddenly he grabbed my hands and looked into my eyes. "As your best friend who loves you more than you'll ever know, I can't just stand by and watch you face this on your own. I know you think you want to push me away. I know you think you want to be alone. I know you think you're in this alone. But you're wrong."

"You're right," I finally said.

"So I'm—what? I'm right?" He was surprised by my admission, and I could tell it was the last thing he'd expected.

"Yeah." I paused, realizing how vulnerable I was feeling. "I've been really lonely lately."

"Clo, you don't have to be lonely."

I nodded.

"Hey, I have a surprise for you."

I raised an eyebrow. "You do? What is it?"

He lifted a bag from beside him and grinned at me. "It's in here."

"Okay…" Confused by what he was about to show me, I watched him take something out of the bag.

"Come on. Sit down on the floor first while I get this set up." I could hear the excitement in his voice.

"Okay, but what are you going to do?" I sat down in the middle of the floor and watched him move around my room.

"You'll see in a minute." He turned off the TV and then my bedroom lamp, leaving only the glow-in-the-dark stars on my ceiling visible in the pitch-black room.

"Okay...do you need me to do anything?" I asked tentatively.

"Yeah, lie down on the floor so you're looking up at the ceiling." I heard him plop himself down on the floor next to me. "I'm going to lie down next to you.

"Okay..." I said again, but this time, I couldn't help but giggle. I wasn't sure what I was expecting, but the anticipation of the surprise temporarily lifted the heaviness that'd been weighing down on my heart.

"You ready?" He said next to me on the floor.

"As ready as I'll ever be."

I heard him click something on.

I gasped at what I saw.

My entire room suddenly glowed with a kaleidoscope of magical lights that moved across the room.

"It's just a rotating disco ball that shines different colors of laser lights. It was the closest thing I could find that might work. It's my version of a—"

"Aurora borealis," I finished his words for him as I stared up at my ceiling in wonder.

"I know it's not the real thing and we're not in glass igloos," he began softly as he looked over at me, "but I really wanted to—"

"Jax," I cut him off with a whisper as I blinked away the hot tears that blinded my eyes. "It's amazing. It's *better* than the real thing." Our eyes met and I hoped that he could see how grateful I was for this moment—how grateful I was for him in my life.

"I'm glad you like it, Clo. I wanted to do something that would make you smile." He spoke in a soft whisper, as if talking louder would make this moment go away.

"Do you know why I love the sky and the stars?" I looked up at the rich glows of reds, blues, and greens dancing across the off-white ceiling filled with stars.

"Why?"

"It's always been amazing to me to know that the magic of the sky and the stars happens every day. It's just beautiful and all around us. Sometimes we just have to take the time to notice something to see how amazing it is."

"You're right." His voice was warm and tender, and from the corner of my eye, I noticed he had turned to look at me. "Once you take notice of that something, you don't know how you'd ever lived without it."

I don't know why, but I felt my cheeks flush at his words.

I turned to look at him, and we shared a smile that caused my heart to skip a beat.

"Thank you, Jax. This was exactly what I needed tonight. I was really lonely."

"Clo, you never have to feel lonely because I'm here for you."

His words touched me in a way I didn't know was possible. "I hope so, Jax. My mom died alone."

"You don't have to hope. I promise."

"Promises can be broken," I whispered as my thoughts went to all the broken promises my mom had made me.

"Not mine, Clo," he said firmly.

I smiled, wanting to believe his every word.

He could tell I was not convinced.

"Clo?"

"Yes?"

"Do you want to make a pact?"

"A pact? What kind of pact?"

He grinned. "How about when we get old, like when we turn thirty or something, and we're still single and not married, we can marry each other? That way, you'll never have to worry about being lonely again."

"Really?" I wasn't sure if he was joking, but the idea of being with Jackson forever made me really happy.

"Yeah, really. We are best friends. We love each other and care about each other."

His words caused my heart to pound against my chest so violently, I wondered if he could hear it.

"Okay," I whispered as we inched closer to each other. "If we're both single when we turn thirty, I'll marry you."

"Deal," he whispered softly. His hand reached for my face and he gently brushed through my hair as he gazed into my eyes. His face sparkled with the myriad of lights that moved across his face, making him look more beautiful than I'd remembered.

I wasn't sure how it happened, but his mouth brushed against mine, and our lips met in a warm, sweet kiss that seemed to melt my insides. It was my first kiss. It was our first kiss. And it was perfect.

Chapter Ten

Present Day

On my flight from Los Angeles to Philadelphia for Clara's wedding, I realized that I had no real friends left in Los Angeles. Carly was the first friend I'd met when I moved to Los Angeles years ago. Then she introduced me to the three other girls in our circle of five girlfriends. After two years, I thought they were as much my friend as they were Carly's. But I was wrong. After I caught Jeff cheating with Carly, none of the girls reached out to me. There were no calls, no emails, no texts. Not even a Google instant message. I had even kept a browser opened to my Gmail account just so I'd always be online and available to chat on Google Talk so they could see me. And I'd seen them online. But no one reached out. It had been radio silence.

It was after the Jeff and Carly incident that I knew for the first time where I stood with them. Apparently it hadn't mattered to them who was in the wrong. Those girls were obviously more Carly's friends than mine.

So, Clara and Sam's wedding couldn't have come at a better time. I needed to get out of Los Angeles and see if I wanted to move back home.

"I'm home," I cried out into the empty hallway from the front doorway of the house.

"We're back here, Co-co," I heard Uncle Tom's voice call out his nickname for me.

I headed in the direction of the kitchen where Uncle Tom's voice had come from.

"Hi!" I greeted them both with hugs and kisses on the cheek. "How are you guys?"

"We're good. Pretty boring now that we've retired," Aunt Betty said with a smile.

I beamed at them. "You guys deserve to relax now."

"So how's everything with you? How's that Jeff guy treating you?"

"We broke up," I said in a matter-of-fact tone. "I'm totally okay with it," I quickly added when I saw the looks of concern on their faces. "He was a jerk."

"Well, I'm sorry that didn't work out for you, honey." Aunt Betty pulled me in for another hug to console me.

"No. Really. It's okay. It happened almost three months ago. Sorry I forgot to mention it during our conversations. I really just didn't want to talk about him."

Aunt Betty nodded in understanding.

"So, what are your plans for your stay here?" Uncle Tom asked, changing the subject. "I hear from your aunt that you're planning on staying for a few months."

"Yeah. I'm thinking about moving back to the area and finding a job in Philly."

"Oh, that's great, honey," Aunt Betty said. "You didn't mention that before."

I smiled, realizing I hadn't told them much about my life since high school. "Sorry I hadn't mentioned it. I actually just decided on it. I only bought a one-way ticket for Clara's wedding because I wasn't sure what I wanted to do." I wasn't about to tell them that I also wanted to see if I could reconnect with Jackson. In fact, I'd never told them that we stopped being friends, and from the way they occasionally brought up

Jackson, it didn't seem like he'd mentioned it to them, either.

"So what about Los Angeles?" There was a worried look on Uncle Tom's face.

"I think it's just not my scene. I subleased my apartment and took three weeks off of work. I figure if I find a job in Philly, I can just quit my job and stay here with you guys for a little while?" I ended my statement in a question and looked over at them sheepishly.

They laughed. "Of course, sweetie," Aunt Betty said right away. "This is your home. You can stay as long as you want."

"Thanks."

"So have you talked to Jackson yet?" Uncle Tom asked.

The mention of his name caused my body to stiffen with a mixture of anxiety and excitement.

"No. Why?"

"Looks like he just got into town last night for the wedding. Did you go over to say hi before coming home?"

I shook my head. "I'll stop by later."

"You should invite him over for dinner sometime," Aunt Betty suggested. "Since his father passed away two years ago, he rarely comes home anymore. It'd be nice to see him. If I remember correctly, he used to love my cooking."

"He really did love your cooking, Aunt Betty. He used to tell me that all the time."

Aunt Betty beamed with pride. "He's a good kid."

"How come you guys never had anything?" Uncle Tom cut in.

"Tom!" Aunt Betty shot him a meaningful look.

"What?" Uncle Tom shrugged. "I've always been curious. They were practically inseparable all the way through high school. And that boy's always had a crush on our Co-Co here."

My breath caught at his words.

Aunt Betty chuckled. "Tom, that's between them. You know kids nowadays have a different way of working through their feelings."

I looked at Aunt Betty. "Do you think that, too? That Jax has always had a crush on me?"

She gave me a warm smile. "Honey, everyone did. Everyone thought you guys liked each other, so we always wondered why you guys stayed just friends."

That afternoon, I let her words sink in and realized how blind I'd been for so long. I'd thought our feelings for each other had developed while we were away at different universities. I thought that'd been when the flirting started. Before college, we kissed each other a few times, but that was it. In high school, we'd both dated other people, though none of those relationships seemed to last more than a few months.

Could Uncle Tom and Aunt Betty be right? Had Jackson liked me for more than just a best friend this entire time, and I hadn't even noticed? As the question marinated in my mind, I became more excited about Clara's upcoming wedding this weekend. Maybe this was what we needed to finally get back to how things used to be between us. Maybe this would be my second chance with him. Maybe he was the one I was meant to be with all along.

***

I didn't know if Jackson was single, but I *did* know that he'd be attending the wedding by himself.

I had called Clara a month ago and casually asked whether Jackson and I would be sitting at the same table. I had RSVP'd without a plus one. She'd confirmed that he would indeed be at my table and proceeded to list the other people who would be sharing our table—something I'd thought she'd do. That was how I knew Jackson also RSVP'd without a plus one to the wedding. When I found out, I had to cover my mouth with my hand so that Clara didn't hear my sheer giddiness at the news. Like Aunt Betty and Uncle Tom, none of my high school friends, including Clara, knew that Jackson and I were no longer friends. At first, I'd been too upset and ashamed to tell anyone that I'd ruined our friendship. I also had no desire for them to know what I'd done. And as time passed, it'd become harder and harder to tell people that we weren't friends anymore. I wasn't sure what Jackson's reasons were, but he never told anyone, either.

After I knew Jackson was attending Clara and Sam's wedding solo, I started preparing myself to see him there. I had planned out what I'd say to him. I had figured out how I'd do my hair and makeup. I had found the perfect sexy, but classy, emerald-green mid-length dress for the wedding. Jackson had once told me I looked the most beautiful in something green. When I'd asked him why, he'd said because it matched the color of his eyes, making us perfect for one another. Now thinking back to that conversation, I wasn't sure how I had been so blind to the fact that he really liked me.

Despite all my preparations to see Jackson at the wedding, what hadn't occurred to me at all, and what I hadn't prepared myself for, was to run smack into him on my morning jog the day before the wedding. Our bodies collided against each other when we both rounded the corner of the street, coming from opposite directions.

"Sorry!" we both said automatically after the impact, but before realizing who we'd run into. But when we took a step away from each other, our eyes met and for a few seconds, we stared at each other in shock.

It'd been nine years since I'd last seen him, and as my eyes took him in, it was clear that age had been very kind to him. He was several inches taller and much more muscular now than he had been in college. With only his running shorts on, my eyes started lingering on his naked muscular pecs. As I watched a few beads of sweat start to drip down his sun-kissed chest, I had an almost uncontrollable urge to run my tongue up along the ridges of his washboard abs. There was no question that he was more handsome and more defined than I'd ever seen him before.

"Hi," I finally said as I tried to recall what I'd wanted to say to him at the wedding tomorrow. I beamed at him, hoping that by some miracle, he had forgiven me and we could put everything behind us without ever having to mention the past.

"Hey." His voice was cold and he didn't return my smile. Instead, he started to move past me, preparing to continue along his jogging path.

"How are you?" I asked. I tried to sound friendly and happy, but my voice came off shrill and an octave higher than normal. But I didn't care, I needed to get a conversation going with him. I needed him to talk to me so that he could forgive me. "Can you believe how long it's been since we've seen each other?" I kept my voice cheerful as I looked at him hopefully.

"Right," he responded flatly, his expression unreadable.

"Nine years, but who's counting?" I forced a laugh, hoping he'd break and laugh back.

But he didn't.

I sighed and gave up my attempts to pretend that nothing was wrong. "Jax—" My voice sounded more pleading.

"Don't call me that, Chloe. There's only one person who used to call me by that nickname, and she doesn't exist anymore."

I flinched in response to both his sharp words and his scathing tone. The fact that he had just called me "Chloe" and not "Clo" also hadn't escaped my notice.

"Can we please sit down and talk about things?" I tried to catch his gaze, but he refused to look at me.

"There's nothing to talk about."

"Yes, there is," I insisted, feeling desperate and frantic. "We need to talk about *us*. Our friendship. Our pact." I cringed the second I heard myself utter those last two words.

He snorted. "Are you serious?"

Feeling a bit flustered, I shook my head. "No," I retracted. "I don't know why that came out."

"Chloe, I gotta run."

"Wait!" I wasn't ready to give up. I wasn't ready to let our first conversation end like this. "I'm sorry, Jax. I'm sorry for what happened. I never meant to hurt you. What happened was such a long time ago. And after everything we've been through, after all those years of being best friends, can you *please* forgive me, Jax?"

He turned away from me and said through gritted teeth, "Just because it was a long time ago, doesn't mean what you did carries less weight."

His words stung, but I still wasn't ready to give up. "Yes, you're right. I made a mistake—a *huge* one. But things have changed. *I've* changed."

He finally turned to face me, and for a mere second, I thought he was finally coming around. But the second his icy stare met my gaze, I knew he hadn't forgiven me. "And I've changed too, Chloe. We've both changed. And that means neither one of us is who we used to be when we were friends."

Without another word, he jogged past me and around the corner, leaving me standing there feeling completely devastated and alone.

Chapter Eleven

Present Day

I almost decided to skip the wedding. As much as I wanted to see Jackson again, I wasn't sure I was emotionally ready for another round of what happened yesterday. But then I realized if I did skip the wedding, he'd know I'd changed my mind last minute; he'd know I was a no-show because of him.

So against all my internal resistance, I arrived at Clara and Sam's wedding in my emerald-green dress, feeling more nervous and less excited about attending the event than I had felt before my run-in with Jackson yesterday.

But to my relief, there were over three hundred guests at the wedding, and I didn't run into Jackson during the ceremony. The wedding was a beautiful outdoor ceremony surrounded by evergreens and lights. Clara and Sam had prepared their own vows and I cried when I watched them share them with each other.

During the wedding ceremony, I was happy to find Cindy and Jules, two other high school friends. It had momentarily calmed my nerves to escape from the constant fear I'd been feeling of unexpectedly running into Jackson at the ceremony.

But I didn't.

I hadn't seen Jackson during the wedding ceremony. I had tried to look around, without looking obvious. But I didn't see him. After the ceremony, I walked with Cindy and Jules to the reception hall where the rest of the night would be held. Cindy and Jules were sitting at a different table, so I had to say goodbye to them before heading to my table.

This time, Jackson was there, sitting at the table by himself.

To my relief, he hadn't seen me yet as I walked in his direction. When I approached the table, I drew in a deep breath to calm my nerves.

"Hi," I said calmly and politely.

I saw his body stiffen at the sound of my voice and my heart sank at his negative reaction to me.

I tried not to let it affect me as I sat down next to him.

We sat there in silence for several minutes without anyone else stopping by our table. Finally, I couldn't stand it any longer and I broke the silence.

"I know I may be the last person you want to talk to, but I just wanted to let you know how sorry I am to hear about the passing of your dad."

"You're right. You're the last person I want to talk to about this."

I shook my head, frustrated by how he'd shut me out.

"How many times do I have to apologize to you?"

"You don't have to apologize at all," he responded without looking at me. "There's really no use in apologizing. What we had is broken, and once it's broken, it's broken—you can't un-break it. There's no way we can change that. An apology can't turn back time to make things different, to make what happened not have happened. An apology doesn't magically let me let go of what's burned into my memory. I can never forget it. So really, you don't have to apologize at all."

I didn't know how to respond to that. It was obvious to me at that point that his hatred for me was still alive and well.

Then he spoke again. "You know there are eight other empty seats you can choose from, why do you insist on sitting right next to me?"

His directness took me by surprise and I had to bite my tongue to stop myself from crying.

I wasn't sure if it was out of spite, or if the drinks with Cindy and Jules earlier had caught up to me, or if I just wanted to speak from the heart, but I turned to him, and answered his question as truthfully as I knew how. "Because you won't talk to me, you won't look at me, and you won't forgive me. Because I miss you. Very much. And every single day. Because for the last nine years, there hasn't been a single day that I didn't hate myself for hurting you. Because I lost my first and only best friend in the world, the man I recently realized that I love and want a life with. And because if I didn't at least tell you all this when I had the chance, there'd be another reason to hate myself every day."

He sat there and looked straight ahead the entire time, but I knew he had heard every word of it.

Upset and frustrated that even after my declaration, where I let myself be vulnerable, he didn't even bother to acknowledge me, I pushed back my chair and ran out of the reception hall in tears.

By the time I got outside, I was sobbing and thinking about going home. Today had been a nightmare and I didn't want to live another second in it.

Just then my phone started to ring in my clutch. I pulled my phone out to see that it was a call from Uncle Tom.

"Hello?"

"Chloe." Something about his voice sounded alarming.

"Uncle Tom, what is it?"

"I know you're at the wedding, but can you leave now?" I knew immediately something was really wrong because he didn't sound like his usual jovial self.

"What's wrong? What's happened?"

"It's Betty," his voiced cracked into a sob. "We're at the hospital."

When I heard the news, it was all too much for me to bear. Everything around me started to spin, making me feel dizzy, and as I saw a figure who looked like Jackson come out of the reception, the world went black.

Chapter Twelve

Spring 2006

Twenty-One Years Old

I had a secret.

It was a secret that no one I cared about knew of.

It was a secret that would change the way those I loved would look at me.

It was a secret that would break Jackson's heart.

So that was why it was the one secret I would take to my grave.

Shortly after I started my freshman year at University of Pennsylvania, because I needed a lot of money—and fast—I was forced to join an elite escort service. It wasn't the typical escort service. In addition to the services a typical escort service would provide, this escort service catered to men who wanted to unleash their wildest fantasies while also maintaining a long-term relationship with the girls they hired. These men wanted the long-term all-inclusive fantasy—the fantasy that they had a hot, young girlfriend or mistress who was willing to fulfill all of their needs, whenever and wherever they wanted.

I had a total of five repeat clients through the service I worked for. For all new clients—those I'd only had regular sessions with for less than twelve months—we would spend our evenings at either their place or hotels. But for my regulars, the clients who treated me like their long-term girlfriends, they also received the added benefit of spending their evenings in the privacy of my condo, which added to the fantasy that I was their girlfriend. Of my five clients, two of them were considered regular clients.

I'd never told Jackson that I was doing this. Since college began, our friendship had changed. I'd felt it, and I think he had too. When we talked on the phone, we'd flirt and talk to each other as if we were boyfriend and girlfriend. I'd never thought of us that way, but lately, the idea of us together, the idea of him loving me in that capacity seemed natural. The more time I would imagine him as my boyfriend, the more I realized I desperately wanted that to be a reality. So the coming weekend was going to be important for us. During our last few conversations, things felt more intimate than before, and I wanted him to be beside me, to kiss me, to make love to me.

Because Jackson was taking the train down from Boston the following night to visit me for the weekend, I had to tell my clients that I wouldn't be available that weekend. So my last scheduled date was that afternoon with one of my regular clients.

As I prepared for my client's arrival, I started taking a few shots of vodka to help loosen me up for the date. When it was almost time for the client's arrival, I slipped on a red lacy slip-grown with matching red lacy panties. I knew it was his favorite, and it got him off faster than my other outfits. I dimmed the lights in my bedroom and turned on the sex music playlist he'd picked out the night before.

Just then I heard the buzzer to my front door. That was his signal to me to get ready. I quickly put on my blindfold securely around my eyes and positioned myself in the center of my bed. The thick blindfold covering my eyes didn't let in even a glimmer of light.

"Come on in!" I called out so he could hear my signal from the door.

I heard the door swing open, and then closed, my lack of vision heightened my sense of hearing.

"Hello?" he called out.

"I'm ready for you in here, baby."

I heard him enter the room and an audible gasp escaped him.

"Do you like what you see? I've been thinking about you all day long and it's gotten me so horny. I need you right now."

"You have?" he asked in a ragged voice.

"Oh yeah. After we talked last night, all I could think about is having you inside of me." I spread my legs wide, revealing myself to him. I could hear his breathing becoming more labored and shallow.

"Come here," I whispered huskily at him.

I felt his hands touch my shoulders and a jolt of electricity shot through me. "Baby, you're really turning me on today." I wondered if I'd had a little too much to drink, because I felt more turned on and wet today than usual.

I felt him kneel down in front of me and I laced my fingers through his hair and pulled him on top of me. His mouth found mine, and I granted him access into my mouth as our tongues crashed together, almost in perfect unison.

I leaned back onto the bed and he followed suit, collapsing on top of me. His lips met with mine again, soft and deep, but with conviction. He reached down to undo his jeans, and I could tell his hands trembled, as my whole body was.

"I've waited so long for this moment," he breathed into my ear before planting a kiss on my cheek.

My heart beat faster as I felt him against me. *Wow, he's ready for me,* and I'd never been this turned on by a client before.

A sudden willingness washed over me, an ability to enjoy whatever he had in store for me. I felt dirty, but suddenly more desirable than ever.

I reached for his hands and pulled them down my inner thigh. Pushing panties to one side, I guided his index finger in and out of me. I gasped and he groaned as we both felt how wet and excited I'd become for him.

"You like that?" I whispered into his ear.

"Very much," he groaned.

"So what do you want to do first to me?"

"Taste you."

Before I realized what he was about to do, I felt his hands pull down my panties and spread my legs apart. Almost immediately, his tongue began to lap me up, causing me to whimper and gasp uncontrollably. I'd never felt this much pleasure before with a client, but for some reason, his hunger was unrelenting as his tongue explored me, causing my body to quiver with such intensity that my entire body tingled and shook.

Then he started to slowly move up my body with his tongue. His hand found my hip, taking its sweet time on a short journey down my thigh. I managed a slight shriek when he began to stroke my inner thigh, deliberately letting his fingers wander higher and higher up my leg. I was overcome with a warmth that began in my belly and spread down my legs. He brought his lips to my ear and began biting at my earring as he spoke to me. *This is a new move for him,* I thought.

His wandering hand found me, stroking the growing wet spot between my legs. I moaned loudly. He thumb teased my throbbing center, tickling it lightly at first, then harder as I began to drip. My screams turned to half-moans as he circled around me harder and harder between my dripping lips until the inevitable warmth began to swell in my clit and intensified at an electrifying rate.

I knew he loved the sound of my screams because he quickly began fingering me, using the all-too-effective "come here" motion. My moans became reduced to raspy breaths as I felt my own warmth running out of me.

"I need you now," I begged. And to my surprise, I meant it.

He began to unzip his pants and I heard him slip on a condom. He removed his hand from between my legs and grabbed my own hand, placing it on his cock.

I gasped at how hard he was and felt him throb in my hand.

I squirmed and pleaded with him through raspy, desperate breaths.

He tore my panties completely off me, pulled up my slip, and began rubbing the tip of his cock on my swollen center. Waves of pleasure surged down my legs again. Just as I felt as though I could take no more, he began to slowly work himself into me, thrusting deeper and deeper, harder and harder, making hardly a sound but for his ragged, heavy breaths.

He began to thrust deeper and deeper, making hardly a sound but for heavy breaths. I couldn't hold on any longer as the friction pushed me off the edge.

"That was incredible! Especially that thing you did at the very end. How come you've never done that before?"

Suddenly, to my surprise, he stopped moving.

"What's wrong?"

"Before? What are you talking about?" There was a familiarity in his voice that seemed out of place.

Suddenly, I felt all the blood drain from my face when I placed that voice. It wasn't my client.

I pulled off my blindfold and my heart stopped at who I saw.

It was Jackson.

"Who did you think I was?" Jackson asked, realizing by my surprised expression that I didn't know it was him I was having sex with.

But before I could try to explain, my client walked through my bedroom door.

"Sorry I'm late, baby. My Viagra kicked in half an hour ago and my cock is so hard for you, I'll need to pay for a double session tonight."

I watched in horror as their eyes met.

Jackson's face went white as anger clouded his eyes. "Dad?"

Author's Note

Thank you for reading *Promise to Marry*, book one in the three-book series *Promises*. Chloe and Jackson's story continues in *Promise to Keep* (book two), which will be out on February 9, 2015 and available on pre-order. The conclusion of their story ends in *Promise of Forever* (book three), which will be out in March 2015.

Thank you for reading *Oblivion*. Please also consider telling your friends and leaving a review for this book. As an indie author, word of mouth and reviews help other readers to discovery my works.

Other Books

If you would like to stay informed of new releases, teasers, and news on my upcoming books, please sign up for Jessica Wood's mailing list or visit me at my website:

http://jessicawoodauthor.com/mailing-list/

http://jessicawoodauthor.com

Below is a list of Jessica Wood's books:

Emma's Story Series

- *A Night to Forget* – Book One
- *The Day to Remember* – Book Two
- *Emma's Story* Box Set – Contains Book One & Book Two

The Heartbreaker Series

This is an *Emma's Story* spin-off series featuring Damian Castillo, a supporting character in *The Day to Remember*. This is a standalone series and does not need to be read with *Emma's Story* series.

- *Damian* – Book One
- *The Heartbreaker* – Prequel Novella to *DAMIAN* – can be read before or after *Damian.*
- *Taming Damian* – Book Two
- *The Heartbreaker Box Set* – Contains all three books.

The Chase Series

This is a standalone series with cameo appearances from Damian Castillo (*The Heartbreaker series*).

- *The Chase, Vol. 1*
- *The Chase, Vol. 2*
- *The Chase, Vol. 3*
- *The Chase, Vol. 4*
- *The Chase: The Complete Series Box Set* – Contains All Four Volumes

Oblivion
This is a standalone full-length book unrelated to other series by Jessica Wood.
- *Oblivion*

***

Pre-Orders Currently Available

- *Promise to Keep* – February 9, 2015

***

<u>Oblivion – Synopsis & Excerpt</u>

SYNOPSIS

I wake up to a life and a man that I can't remember.

He says his name is Connor Brady—the tall, sexy CEO of Brady Global, Inc.

He says my name is Olivia Stuart, and that I was recently in an accident and lost my memory.

Also, he says I'm his fiancé.

Although I don't remember Connor, or anything about my past, something about him seems familiar. He is kind, protective, and breathtakingly-gorgeous. But there is just one problem—he seems *too* perfect.

As I begin to rebuild my relationship with Connor and accept the idea that I may never remember my past, I unexpectedly meet Ethan James.

Ethan is the mysterious, rebellious stranger who pushes my boundaries to their limits and makes me feel alive. As our lives collide time and time again, the bits and pieces of my past start to unravel, unearthing the secrets that have been buried deep inside my subconscious. With every new memory I gain about who I once was, I become more torn between the man who is my fiancé and the stranger who is the key to my past. Is my life with Connor really as perfect as he leads me to believe?

CHAPTER ONE

Tears streamed down my face as I ran into my bedroom and slammed the door behind me. I reached for my diary—the familiar pink leather journal that was filled with my deepest thoughts. My shaky fingers pulled the gold fabric ribbon page marker, taking me to my last entry, and I began to frantically scribble down everything I was feeling at that moment—all the pain and fear that raced inside me as the screaming escalated an octave higher between my parents outside of my room.

They're fighting again. It's been happening more and more frequently, each time worse than the day before.

I wish they weren't so unhappy. I wish my parents didn't hate each other so much. I wish I was anyone else but myself right now. I wish I was anywhere else but here.

As if hearing my thoughts, I heard my father roar, "If you want a fucking divorce, you can have it! But I'm going to warn you just this once: if you walk out of that door, don't ever think about coming back again!"

"I don't plan on it!" I heard my mother spit back. "I'm leaving first thing tomorrow, and I'm taking Liv with me!"

"No!" I cried, my mind racing as I thought about everything I was about to lose.

Just then, my room and the pink leather diary in my hand faded away into the background as my consciousness registered a soft, steady beeping in the distance. *What is that?*

When I turned toward the sound, I found myself running across a familiar street in the middle of the night. I was wearing a jewel-encrusted blush-pink evening gown that weighed down on my body and restricted my movement. The air was bitter cold and cutting, but the adrenaline that coursed inside me seemed to shelter me from the cold like a numbing blanket.

Suddenly, I saw two bright, blinding headlights coming toward me at high speed. The sharp screeching of car tires filled the air, drowning out all other noise. I felt the impact of cold *metal against my body as I was lifelessly flung sideways against the solid pavement.*

I braced myself for the impact of the pain that would greet my body.

But it didn't come.

Instead, the steady beeping returned, but this time, it seemed closer, louder.

Then a hushed conversation seeped through my consciousness.

"There's nothing we can do for her right now, Mr. Brady. As you know she has suffered some head injuries from the accident, so all we can do right now is to wait for her to wake up and see from there." The female voice seemed miles away, but for some reason, I knew she was talking about me.

"Okay. Thank you." The man's voice was strained and low as I heard him walk in my direction.

I felt my head throb in pain, in time with that unnerving beeping that became increasingly louder.

"She's very lucky to have someone like you to visit and be by her side every day. You must really care about her."

"Yeah. I do." The male voice was closer than before.

Then I felt a warm hand on mine, bringing me into the present. My mind registered the bed I was lying on. The smell of stale, chlorine air invaded my senses. The beeping came into focus and I could hear it coming from a machine a foot away from me. *Am I in a hospital?*

My fingers twitched as I tried to move my body.

"Nurse!" the man's voice cried out in alarm. "I think I felt her move."

My eyes fluttered open and closed, struggling against the heaviness of my lids and the blinding lights that stung my eyes.

"I think she's waking up!" The man squeezed my hand as he inched closer to my face. "Liv?"

"Mr. Brady, let's give her some room." The man loosened his grip on me and I heard him move away.

I opened my eyes again, and this time, it was easier. My vision was blurred as I looked around, but I could detect two figures close by.

"Ms. Stuart?" The female voice was gentle as she moved toward me.

"Where am I?" I blinked and after a couple of seconds, her face came into focus. "Who are you?" I looked around the room and found myself in a surprisingly large and luxurious hospital room.

"Ms. Stuart, you were in an accident and you're at The Pavilion, a private in-patient hospital unit at the University of Pennsylvania hospital. I'm Nurse Betty and I've been taking care of you."

"An accident." I repeated her words and tried to think through the dense fog consuming my every thought. Then I winced at the throbbing pain in my head.

"Are you in any pain?" She looked at me with concern.

"Just a horrible headache." I reached for my head.

"I'll let the doctor know and we'll get you something for that."

"What happened to me?" I looked up at her, searching her face for answers.

She flashed me a kind smile. "There's actually someone that's been here waiting for you to wake up for quite some time. I'll let him tell you what happened while I check your vitals." She moved aside and my eyes focused on the other figure in the room—the tall, handsome man in a tailored charcoal suit standing anxiously behind her.

"Hi." I looked at him, unsure of what else to say to this stranger.

"Liv? Thank God you finally woke up."

I smiled at him. His warm, hazel eyes were filled with concern as he moved in front of the nurse to grab my hand. I studied him, wondering why he seemed so familiar.

He reached for me. Deep creases formed between his brows as he furrowed them in worry. "Liv, how are you feeling?" His voice was smooth and gentle. I couldn't quite place where, but I knew I'd heard it before.

I placed my hands to my head and groaned. "Besides this killer headache, I'm okay." I tried to get up but my arms felt weak as I slumped back down against the pillows when I tried to sit up. He reached over and helped me lean up against the headboard of the bed.

"It's so good to see you awake." He held my face and kissed me gently on my forehead.

I flinched and frowned up at him. "Who are you? Have we met before?"

His expression changed immediately and he whipped around and turned to the nurse. I saw them exchange a look that I didn't understand.

He then turned back to me and frowned, his eyes filled with sadness. "You don't remember me?"

I studied his face and thought about it. "No, I don't think so," I finally said as I shook my head.

"What's the last thing you remember?" he asked me tentatively. I didn't need to know this man to detect the anxious expression on his face.

I stared at him and tried to rack my brain, searching for anything I could remember. I shook my head in frustration as I buried it in my hands. My head was pounding in pain as if I had just awoken from the worst hangover of my life.

"Liv, are you okay? What's wrong?" The alarm in his voice exacerbated the panic that was building inside.

"Why do you keep calling me Liv?" I felt annoyed as I looked back up at him. My annoyance turned to worry when I saw the shocked expression on his face.

The nurse stepped forward. "Do you remember your name?"

I opened my mouth, ready to answer her simple question, but then stopped. It was only then, when I was forced to think about it, that it dawned on me that I didn't actually know the answer. "I...I can't remember."

"Is there anything you do remember?" Her tone was gentle and cautious.

I searched my thoughts, trying to grab onto any memory. But everything outside the last few minutes seemed like a dream that I had somehow forgotten the moment I woke up. *Why can't I remember anything?* I shook my head in frustration. "What happened to me?"

"I'll let Mr. Brady here tell you what happened while I go get Dr. Miller."

"Honey, I'm Connor. Connor Brady. Are you sure you don't remember me?" The man moved back toward me, a mixture of hopefulness and uncertainty painted across his face.

"Connor," I repeated in a monotone voice. I studied him, trying to place him to some moment in my life. There was something about him that was familiar, but as hard as I tried, I couldn't seem to remember how I knew him. I shook my head slowly. "I don't even remember my own name."

"Your name is Olivia Stuart. Your friends call you Liv." He sat down on the chair next to my bed and placed his hand on top of mine. His hand was warm and familiar but it felt weird to have this stranger touching me in this intimate way. I didn't pull my hand away, though. I needed answers and this man seemed to have them, so the last thing I wanted to do was to offend him.

"What happened to me?"

His face fell. "You were in a hit-and-run accident." His voice cracked and he cleared his throat. He paused before continuing. "You've been in a coma for the past eight days since the accident."

Panic and confusion swirled around me at the idea of losing so much time without knowing it. "Eight days? But…but I don't remember any of this. Why can't I remember anything?" I felt frantic as I tried to push through the fog and my mind came back blank.

"Liv, you sustained some head injuries from the accident. The doctors said that memory loss was a possibility when you woke up…"

I stared at him in disbelief as my hands immediately moved up to my head. When my fingers traced the layers of bandages, I knew he was telling me the truth.

"Don't worry. The doctors say that if there's memory loss, it might only be temporary," he tried to reassure me. "You might slowly regain your memories back."

"Might?" I didn't feel reassured by that word.

Just then a middle-aged bald man in a white lab coat walked into the room. A warm smile appeared on his friendly face. "Ms. Stuart. I'm Dr. Miller. It's great to see you awake. How are you feeling?"

"What's wrong with me, Dr. Miller? Why can't I remember who I am?"

"Let me ask you a few questions first, alright?"

"Okay."

"Do you know when you were born?"

I searched my mind, trying to recall the answer. Nothing. I shook my head.

"Do you know where you went to high school?"

"No." I shook my head again as I felt the frustration and helplessness grow inside.

"Do you know the name of Philadelphia's football team?"

To my surprise, I didn't draw a blank this time. "The Eagles."

"You remember," Connor said excitedly as he squeezed my hand.

Dr. Miller smiled. "Can you tell me how many states there are in the U.S.?"

"Fifty." I frowned at the doctor, wondering if that was a trick question. "There are a few territories like Puerto Rico and Guam though," I added.

"Well, it looks like you've suffered from some memory loss due to the accident, but not all. It's not uncommon for someone to have some degree of amnesia after a traumatic event like the one you experienced. From your answers, it appears the amnesia has affected your episodic memory, which is the memory of experiences and specific events—the memories personal to you. But it seems that the amnesia didn't affect your semantic memory, which is the memory dealing with facts and your knowledge of the eternal world." He studied the clipboard in his hands. "The good news is from all the tests we've run on you, it doesn't seem like there was any damage to the areas of your brain that store your long-term memories."

"What does that mean, doctor?" the handsome man in the charcoal suit cut in to ask.

"Well it should mean that Ms. Stuart hasn't suffered any long-term memory loss."

"So I don't understand. Why can't I remember anything about myself, then?"

"That's the thing we don't know at this time. The brain is a miraculous and mysterious thing. It's unlikely that you're suffering from any permanent brain damage."

"So what's the problem?" Connor asked, his grip tightened around my hand.

"Sometimes the brain will suppress memories after going through a traumatic experience. That memory hasn't been forgotten in the traditional sense, but it's locked away by the sub-conscious and removed from the conscious mind."

"So does that mean I'll get my memories back?" I looked at him hopefully.

"The chances are good, but it's also not a guarantee either that you'll get some or all of your memories back. The best thing for you is to go back to your life before the accident and surround yourself with the things that are familiar and important to you—those are usually the things that will help trigger your memories."

"Liv, baby, I promise to help you through this." Connor held up my hand between both of his as he pulled it close to his chest. He looked up at Dr. Miller. "Doc, what's the next step?"

"Well Ms. Stuart, since you just woke up from the coma, I'd like to run some tests and keep you under careful observation at the hospital for a week or so. During this time, you'll also start your physical therapy to strengthen your muscles that have been inactive while you've been here. If the tests look good, then we can have you released as early as next week."

"Thank you, doctor. That's good news." Connor beamed at me.

But as much as I tried, I couldn't seem to adopt his excitement.

Sensing my unease, his expression changed. "What's wrong, honey?"

As if taking this as a signal, the doctor cleared his throat. "Ms. Stuart, we'll let you guys talk. I'll check up on you in an hour or so to run those tests."

Anxiety built inside me as I watched the doctor and nurse slip out of the room. Even though I knew that this man in the charcoal suit seemed to know who I was, he still felt like a stranger to me, and being completely alone with him made me uneasy.

"What are you thinking, Liv?" he finally broke the silence.

"Liv...Olivia." I said my name aloud. It sounded foreign, yet familiar from my mouth. I then met Connor's gaze. He smiled at me as he studied my expression. "I still don't know who you are exactly. I mean, I know your name is Connor, but...how do we know each other?"

His smile disappeared and I saw the sadness in his eyes again. "Liv, I'm your fiancé."

"Fiancé?"

He nodded. I followed his gaze as it darted down to my left hand. To my surprise, there on my ring finger was a large, sparkling diamond set on top of a platinum, diamond-encrusted eternity band. *How did I not see this earlier?*

I looked back at him in silence, overwhelmed by everything.

"This must be a lot for you to take in right now. And I'm sure you have a lot of questions. I'll be happy to answer whatever I know. Let's just take this one step at a time. We can go at the pace you're most comfortable with, okay?"

I nodded and drew in a deep breath as thousands of questions whirled around in my head, fighting for my attention.

"Thanks." I gave him a small smile, grateful for his patience and understanding. At that moment I thought about how hard this must be for him as well—to be engaged to and in love with someone who doesn't remember you or feel that same love anymore.

"Can we take this slowly? I just feel really overwhelmed."

"Of course, Liv. I understand. Whatever you need. Just tell me what you want. Okay?"

I nodded again. "Who are my parents? Do I have any siblings? Do they know I'm here?"

I saw the pained expression on Connor's face and knew I wouldn't like the answer.

"I'm sorry, Liv. Your mom passed away a few years ago. You don't have any siblings."

"Did you know my mom? What kind of person was she?" Tears streamed down my face as I felt the loss for the mother I couldn't remember.

"She passed away right before we met here in Philly. I believe you left New Jersey and moved here to start a new life."

"Oh. And my dad?"

He shook his head. "You rarely talked about him. From the little you have said, you haven't seen him since you were thirteen—"

"—when my parents got a divorce…" I finished his comment as I remembered the flashback I had right before I woke up.

"Yeah." Connor looked at me in alarm. "Are you remembering things?"

"Maybe. I had a flashback of them fighting when I was young right before I woke up."

"Oh. Did you get any other flashbacks?"

"I don't know. I think a little bit from the accident."

"Oh?"

"Yeah. I think I was running across the street and then a car came toward me and hit me."

"I'm so sorry, Liv." Connor buried his face in his hands. "It's all my fault."

"What do you mean? Were you driving that car?" I looked at him in alarm.

"No, of course not!" He shook his head. "I…I just feel responsible for you."

I frowned. I could tell there was something he wasn't telling me. "Do you know how my accident happened? Were you there?"

He nodded and looked away. "I wish I could take it all back. I wish…"

"What happened? Please tell me."

He looked up at me and I saw the regret in his face. "It was the night of our engagement party at the Franklin Institute Science Museum." His eyes glazed over and he smiled as his thoughts took him back to that night. "You looked absolutely gorgeous in that jeweled gown." He paused and his expression turned somber. "At some point during the night, you went out to the front of the museum. That's when the car hit you."

"I remember running across the street when the car hit me," I said slowly as I thought back to the flashback I had right before I woke up. I stared at him, trying to remember more from that night. *How come it's so hard to remember?* I thought in frustration.

"I'm so sorry, Liv. I should have been there for you. Maybe if I were there, this wouldn't have happened…"

I frowned, trying to figure out how to comfort this man who seemed to be consumed with guilt. "You didn't know this was going to happen." I saw the anguish in his eyes and reached for his hand to reassure him. "It's not your fault."

"But it did happen." I saw his body stiffen and knew it wasn't going to be easy for him to forgive himself.

"Connor, please don't."

He looked up at me with pained eyes.

"There's nothing you could've done differently when you didn't know. I wish I had my memories. I wish I hadn't been running across the street when the car came. I wish things were different." I blinked away a tear. "But sometimes we don't always get what we wish for. Sometimes we can only work with the hand that we're dealt." I was surprised by the sudden acceptance I felt for what had happened. *Maybe those who say, "ignorance is bliss," are right.*

"Is there anything I can do to help?"

I looked at this stranger and somehow I knew I would remember him again. I knew he was important to me. I looked down at the engagement ring on my finger and instantly felt a loss for all the special memories that I didn't have anymore.

"What's wrong, Liv?" He saw the fresh tears in my eyes that were threatening to make their way down my cheeks.

"It's just a lot to take in all at once."

"I know."

I watched him gently brush the tears from my cheeks, and from the way his hands caressed my face, I knew he'd touched me many times before. *Were we happy before this accident? What kind of person was I when we were together? What did I enjoy doing?* It wasn't until then that another question hit me like a ton of bricks. *What do I look like?*

I gave him a weak smile. "Connor, I'm really tired. I'd like some time alone to digest all this."

His brows furrowed with worry but he didn't try to object. "Okay." He got up from the chair and looked down at me. "I'll stop by first thing tomorrow morning to see you."

"Okay." I forced a small smile.

He leaned down toward me and kissed me gently on my forehead. "I'll see you tomorrow. I love you, gorgeous," he whispered.

As I watched him leave, the hospital room suddenly disappeared.

For a split second I found myself in a grand, sun-drenched bedroom lying naked on a large luxurious bed under lush layers of satin sheets. I screamed out and my back arched upward as intense pleasure radiated throughout my body. I felt a pair of strong, rough hands grip my thighs tightly, keeping them spread apart as a long and hard tongue plunged in and out of me, pushing me to the brink of my release. After I came, I felt another naked body move up my body from somewhere under the layers and a second later, Connor's face emerged out from under the sheets. He flashed me a wicked smirk as he slowly licked his lips. "And that's how much I love you, gorgeous."

I gasped at the memory that had just hit me, and my body tingled as if that moment had just happened. I looked down at my body and the question that had blindsided me a few minutes earlier crossed my mind again. *What do I look like?*

I slowly got up from the bed, and felt my muscles weak from the days of being on the hospital bed. It took me several minutes to move to the bathroom where there was a full-length mirror along the wall facing the door.

Standing in front of the mirror was like standing face to face with a complete stranger. Nerves prickled through my body like ice, cold needles as I studied every inch of the unfamiliar person in front of me. Nothing about my reflection looked familiar. Her radiant blue eyes stared back at me. Even through the bandages around her forehead, I could see the long wavy blond hair that cascaded down the curves of her small frame. I watched as this stunning woman staring back at me touched her face with both hands. I felt her fingers move across my face.

"I'm Olivia Stuart." My whispered words filled the silent room and seemed to hang in the air as I continued to study myself in the reflection. *Will this ever stop feeling so strange?*

***

After a week at the hospital and focusing on my physical therapy, I felt slightly better and hopeful about everything. The tests Dr. Miller had ran all came out normal and I was cleared to leave today.

"Hey, gorgeous."

I looked up to find Connor at my door with a large bouquet of pink roses.

"Hi." I smiled, happy to see a familiar face. "You're back."

"Of course I'm back, silly. I've been visiting you every day, and every day you seem surprised to see me. Are you trying to get rid of me or something?"

I could see from his smile that he was joking, and I giggled uneasily. "No, that's not what I mean." I wasn't sure how to tell him that the reason I seemed surprised to see him was because to me, he felt like a stranger.

"Well, like it or not, I'm here to take you home today, like I'd promised."

"Oh, right." Our eyes met and I felt my stomach flip nervously. I immediately looked away and felt my face turn beet red when I remembered my flashback of the intense orgasm this man had given me. I knew that for him, we were lovers in love, but for me, I felt embarrassed and exposed that this handsome stranger knew me more intimately than I knew myself.

"What's wrong?" He walked over to me and kissed me lightly on my cheek.

"Nothing." I pushed my thoughts aside and flashed him a smile.

He handed me the bouquet in his hands. "Pink roses are your favorite."

"Thank you. They're beautiful." I took the stunning bouquet and was instantly hit with its intoxicating smell.

"How are you feeling?"

"Better," I responded honestly.

"Good. So are you ready to blow this popsicle stand then?"

I let out a light chuckle and nodded.

Thirty minutes later, Connor had helped me finish all my paperwork to check out of the hospital. I had changed into a white Splendid cotton silk tee, dark-washed J Brand jeans, and a pair of black Christian Louboutin patent leather stilettos that Connor brought for me from my closet. According to him, this was one of my favorite casual outfits. I had stared dubiously at the three-inch heels when he had handed them to me. They looked more painful than comfortable to me. But when I put them on, they had hugged my feet perfectly and I was surprised by how at ease I was walking around in them.

"Hey, gorgeous." Connor looked up from the hospital paperwork when I walked out of the bathroom. "You look like you're back to your old self." I watched as his eyes moved up and down my body, and a nervous shiver ran down my back.

"I guess my muscle memory's still intact," I joked as I looked at my heels.

He chuckled and shook his head. "I never did understand how you could walk in those things. You know on one of our first dates, I called you Wonder Woman when I saw you running in a pair just like those."

I smiled. "Why was I running?"

"We had just had an amazing date at Tria, this great wine bar in the city, and you had a few glasses too many." He smiled as he told the story. "Well, by the end of the night, you were running and skipping down the street without a care in the world and giggling uncontrollably." He laughed at the memory and beamed at me. "It was at that moment that I knew I'd fall in love with you."

I laughed along with him, wishing I could remember that memory, wishing I could remember how it had felt to possibly share those same feelings toward him.

A few minutes later we were outside, standing at the entrance of the hospital.

"Liv, I'm going to go get the car. You okay with waiting right here for me? I'll bring the car around and pick you up."

I nodded and smiled. He's such a gentleman.

He leaned in and kissed me gently on the forehead. "I love you, gorgeous."

"Thanks." I cringed inside as soon as the word came out. I wasn't sure what to say. I had a feeling he wanted more, but telling a stranger I loved him wasn't something I was ready to give.

He gave a light chuckle and smiled. "I'll be back."

As I watched him walk away and turn the corner toward the entrance of the parking garage, I was preoccupied with thoughts of how the following days, weeks, and months would be for us.

Suddenly I heard people approach me from the left.

"Excuse me! Please make way!"

I turned and saw a couple barreling toward me. It was a man holding up a pregnant woman who appeared to be in a lot of pain. "My wife's water broke! Please move!"

I finally realized that I was standing in the middle of the hospital entrance and blocking their path. I hastily took a step back to give them room to pass me, but it was too late. The man pushed past me and as I took a step back, my heel caught on a crack in the pavement and I lost my balance and fell backward.

Just as I thought I was about to hit the ground, a strong arm caught me from behind and pulled me up. I gasped in surprise at my near-fall and found myself tightly clutched within someone's protective arms.

"Careful there or you're going to hurt yourself in those killer heels."

I looked up and let out an audible gasp as my gaze locked with a pair of intensely-dark, smoldering brown eyes staring down at me.

If you enjoyed this excerpt from *Oblivion*, a completely standalone full-length book, the book is currently available.

About the Author

Jessica Wood writes new adult contemporary romance.

While she has lived in countless cities throughout the U.S., her heart belongs to San Francisco. To her, there's something seductively romantic about the Golden Gate Bridge, the steep rolling hills of the city streets, the cable cars, and the Victorian-style architecture.

Jessica loves a strong, masculine man with a witty personality. While she is headstrong and stubbornly independent, she can't resist a man who takes control of the relationship, both outside and inside of the bedroom.

She loves to travel internationally, and tries to plan a yearly trip abroad. She also loves to cook and bake, and—to the benefit of her friends—she loves to share. She also enjoys ceramics and being creative with her hands. She has a weakness for good (maybe bad) TV shows; she's up-to-date on over 25 current shows, and no, that wasn't a joke.

And it goes without saying, she loves books—they're like old and dear friends who have always been there to make her laugh and make her cry.

The one thing she wished she had more of is time.

If you would like to follow or contact Jessica Wood, you can do so through the following:

Mailing List: http://jessicawoodauthor.com/mailing-list/

Blog: http://jessicawoodauthor.com

Facebook: www.facebook.com/jessicawoodauthor

Twitter: http://twitter.com/jesswoodauthor

Pinterest: http://pinterest.com/jessicawooda/

8533

Made in the USA
Lexington, KY
04 June 2015